FRANK

ECE GURLER

To Adina
With Love
Ece Gurler
11.29.2020

Text copyright © 2020 by Ece Gurler
Illustration copyright © 2020 by Ece Gurler and Ujala Shahid

First paperback edition 2020

ISBN (Print Edition): 978-1-09832-011-9
ISBN (eBook Edition): 978-1-09832-012-6

Printed in Pennsauken, NJ, U.S.A.

CuriousTurk
Boston, Massachusetts 02130

Table of Contents

Dedicated to my brother, Ege Gurler, who has always been there for me with his endless support and love...

"*For small creatures such as we, the vastness is bearable only through love.*"

— *Carl Sagan*

1

FRANK

It was three weeks until Christmas. For the first time that winter, it had been snowing non-stop the whole day. As he always did when he saw the snow, Frank ran to the window, put his elbows in the window pane, placed his chubby cheeks in between his hands, and looked at the snow. He could hear the cold wind forcing its way through the window frame. His eyes were wide open. His huge glasses slid farther down his nose when he approached even closer to the window to see the single snow flake that landed in front of him. *Wow!* he thought to himself, amused, *everything is symmetrical! So cool!* He cracked open the window and tried to catch some flakes but they melted as soon as they landed on his hands. The cold air rushed in and the wind was filling in his room. His glasses were all fogged up now so it was impossible to see the flakes.

"Frank! Dinner is ready!" his mother yelled from downstairs.

"I'm coming!" Frank replied.

He quickly closed the window and jumped onto his bed. He grabbed his tablet which had been sitting on his nightstand not for more than a few minutes long. He said to himself excitedly, "I still have ten percent charge, good! Enough for me to check out some cool shapes of snowflakes!" Then he typed, 'Why snowflakes are symmetrical' in the search tab and so many links were listed. He scrolled up and down, trying to skim for the best possible information with amazing pictures, opening every link that he liked on a different tab. "Why is it taking so long to load the page? Ugh!" he muttered.

"Frank! I said it is dinner time! You know what we talked about this morning!" His mother sounded louder this time.

The morning conversation with his mom had included something like his father got mad or something when Frank didn't show up on time for breakfast. He called him lazy and said he needed to be more responsible. Of course, he didn't know that Frank was spending his morning reading about how birds never get lost during their migration because of earth's magnetic field. Anyway, he didn't want to make his parents mad so left his tablet carefully back on his night stand, turned the light off and yelled back to his mother, "I'm coming!"

Frank loved his parents. His mother was always kind and caring with him. She would always try to help Frank with his homework, and most of the time even though not needing her help, he acted like he did. He just loved her being around him, showing affection and love. She would come home tired from work but when she saw Frank her face would light up all of a sudden. She would open her arms wide and kneel down to get a hug from Frank. She would kiss him, cuddle him, and ask him how his day had been.

His father, on the other hand, was not his best friend, for sure. Because he wouldn't let Frank watch TV after 08:00 PM, and he wasn't a big fan of sleepovers. He had so many rules and was always so proud of them. But despite everything, Frank knew that his father loved him. One morning, while coming downstairs for breakfast, he had overheard that they didn't have enough money to pay the bills. Both his mom and dad looked so upset. When he came into the kitchen Frank acted like he hadn't heard anything. The very same day, though, his father picked him up after school, and when Frank got in the car, there it was sitting on the black leather seat, his favorite science magazine! Frank started going through the pages so enthusiastically that he didn't even hear his father talking to him.

"Frankie, you forgot to close your door, boy!" His father laughed.

Frank grinned, "Oops, sorry!" and closed the door. "Thank you, Dad!" he smiled at his dad through the rearview mirror.

Their eyes met. "You are welcome." His father smiled back. "Come on, put on your seat belt now."

Frank never understood why his father had stopped working a while ago. He used to work for this repair shop with Uncle

Dave and suddenly he stopped going to work. He had been at the house for a while and seemed upset almost all the time. Frank didn't understand why his dad had to yell at him for little things, like when he forgot to brush his teeth or take the trash out. Anyone could forget things. For example, this kid in school, Martin, would always forget his math book at home. Their teacher never raised her voice at him.

Frank's father never used to yell at him. At all. He remembered last Christmas being so much fun. Frank and his father had watched this space documentary together, and after that as the tradition follows, he made little planet cookies with his mother. He remembered that he had wanted to color Jupiter green but they were out of green food coloring. Seeing Frank so sad, his father had brought some mint ice-cream and spread it over the cookie. "Here you go, you have your green Jupiter! Now, eat it, before the ice-cream melts." The cookies were so delicious, and everything felt perfect that day. In fact, Frank was the happiest kid in the world last Christmas. But this Christmas was different. He didn't think there would be any planet cookies or documentaries. Because his mother was supposed to work, looking after some rich family's kids. Also, his father seemed too sad to watch anything fun with him.

"Are you going to eat or keep digging until you find a gold mine there, hon?" said his mother, jokingly.

Frank looked at her across the table and said, "I don't think I'm hungry, Mom."

She looked at him worried. "I thought you loved my chicken pot pie?"

"Yes, I do, Mom. Really. I just don't feel like eating. They had my favorite chicken nuggets for lunch today. I think I ate more than I should have. Can I go upstairs and read, mom, please?"

His mother sighed heavily and put her head down. She grabbed her neck with her hand gently, then she lifted her head and looked right at Frank. "Your father will get upset when he hears you are not eating dinner, you know that, right?" she asked. Frank could see the frown lines appeared between her eyebrows.

Frank looked at his food on the table and muttered to himself, "He is always upset these days anyways." He was sure that his mother heard what he said, and he regretted saying it right away, but it was too late anyway.

She got up, grabbed his plate. "OK. Go upstairs, but do your homework first before you read anything on that tablet, do you hear me?"

"OK. Mom," Frank said. He ran to the stairway while his mom started the water running for the dishes. Then, for some reason Frank came back to the kitchen, not sure why, maybe to say thank you to his mom. But he didn't say anything. He just looked at her and watched her. Her dark brown hair was draped over her shoulders gracefully. Her green dress reminded Frank of the new fact he had learned in biology class about photosynthesis. What it means is that green plants use the sunlight to turn the carbon dioxide in the air into their food. He was amazed when he learned after photosynthesis, both oxygen and carbohydrates were produced. While she had her back turned at him, for some reason Frank could feel her. He thought, *how come we can tell someone looks tired, without even seeing their faces?*

Frank went upstairs thinking about his homework. He had to write an essay on "The Importance of Teamwork." But he didn't know how to start. He had never liked social sciences. They were pointless to him, it wasn't even "exact science." When there was a science paper due, he would finish them in less than an hour. But with sociology, he struggled. He was aware that he wasn't able to grasp some things that other people could see or understand. He never knew why. For example, one time in a group project, Frank and his teammates were presenting to the class about natural selection. At the end of the presentation, the class was allowed to ask questions to the group. Frank answered all twelve questions himself because he knew all the answers. After that day, his teammates stopped talking to him. When he confronted Jim, one of the kids in the project group, he said what Frank did was rude because he jumped at every question and didn't let others take a part. Frank was puzzled hearing this. He truly tried to understand but he couldn't. Yes, there were questions asked and, in the end, they were answered accurately. That was what mattered, wasn't it? Why was it important who told them? *Why was it a big deal?*

Frank didn't have any friends at school. But he had one close friend, Ramzi, the neighbor boy. They would play video games and eat pizza sometimes. Ramzi was also into space stuff. That's why Frank really liked hanging out with him. Frank guessed Ramzi didn't have any other friends, either. Otherwise, why would he hang out with Frank?

The sociology essay was supposed to be five hundred words, but Frank was stuck at two hundred and three. He had been staring at the half-blank document for about twenty minutes, doing nothing. His brain was trying to avoid homework, so he thought about things like, *if I had a dog, I would name him Proton. Or, Newton! After Isaac Newton. Yes, that is a better name! Oh, I should have eaten dinner, I'm hungry now. Mom will get mad.* In the midst of these wandering thoughts, he heard his father coming home and shutting the door. *Good!* Frank thought, *when he comes upstairs to check up on me, he will see that I'm working on my homework! Maybe then he can get me that blue star bike I always wanted for Christmas!*

But Dad didn't come upstairs. In a couple of minutes, Frank heard his mother and father arguing about something. It got louder and louder, to the point that Frank couldn't concentrate on his paper anymore. He left his chair with curiosity and opened his door just a little bit to hear what they were saying. He heard his mom saying something like, "I can't be the only one working in this house anymore!" and his father yelled, "Don't you think I'm trying here, woman!"

Frank closed his door quietly. This was yet another big argument of many in the last months. Unfortunately, it had become their evening habit now. They used to get along so well; Frank didn't understand what had changed. But it seemed like they fight almost every day now. He decided to take a break and go to his Aurora Shell, as he always would do when his parents had a fight or when he wanted to feel better.

2

AURORA SHELL

Aurora Shell was more than a closet. When you opened the two white wooden doors, it would reveal a secret world full of fun. Inside was wide enough to fit four seated people. In the left corner, he had a huge pile of stacked science magazines. The oldest one was from almost three years ago. Next to the pile, there were his *Star Wars* action figures standing aligned on the beige carpet. His collection had only ten characters so far, but he was content with that number. They were lined up in order from his least favorite character on the left, *Emperor Palpatine*, to his favorite character on the very right, *Yoda*. He never understood why people liked *Darth Vader*. He wasn't wise, and Frank thought he was always grumpy. Frank didn't like angry people. Like today, he disliked his dad the most.

The wall in Aurora Shell was covered in posters. They weren't posters of pop stars or football players though. They didn't involve any cars, either. The biggest one was pinned at the very center – the periodic table of elements. Above that there was a smaller size picture of the Milky Way, and the left most one was a poster of *HMS Beagle*, the ship that Charles Darwin traveled the world with to study natural history. On the left side of the wall, there was this old poster of the Big Bang theory. Frank always wondered how from nothing we had suddenly had this house, this city and the solar system. It was so cool for him to think about it.

When opening the closet doors and passing through his hanging clothes, before you saw these posters, there was something else that would catch your eye: little globes hanging from the ceiling. The Solar System. He had made all those globes in his science class project using foam balls, glue and paint. Oh, what an exciting day it was! He'd been careful about the scale and everything. He'd made sure that the diameter ratios would make sense. There was a tiny problem though. The project was missing the Sun because he couldn't find the exact yellow tone that he'd wanted in the store. After he put the solar system up in the closet, he sat on the floor in the middle of everything where the Sun was supposed to be. He looked up. Suddenly, he felt so powerful. Everything was going to rotate around him now. He was in control, like the captain of the ship *HMS Beagle*. Whenever he felt lonely or frustrated, this was the place that would make him the happiest, the center of his Aurora Shell. So that whenever he felt like he lost control of his life, he could take it back right in here.

Besides the bright white light of his tablet, there was one more thing lighting up the darkness in this shell: a small white box of LED light that projects lights, sitting on the pile of his science magazines. When you pushed its little red button, it would project these unbelievably beautiful lights of different colors on his wall – red, blue and green – like the lights of the Aurora Borealis, all slowly but constantly moving.

Aurora borealis – also known as Northern Lights – can only be seen in certain areas of the world. His lights looked so beautiful that he sometimes would forget to read. He would sit on the cushions in the right corner, stretch his legs and take his favorite position: he would cross his hands behind his head and cross his legs. He would watch the lights moving from one wall to another tirelessly, dreaming of seeing the real ones one day.

Frank never thought about why he called this place a *shell*. But he had read in many books that when the snails and turtles got scared or felt unsafe, they would just leave the outside world and go back into their shells to protect themselves and recover. He thought, *maybe that is why I call it Aurora Shell! It is my happy and safe place.*

3

THE TRUTH

Christmas was just one week away, and still Frank hadn't seen any gifts under the Christmas tree. This was very unusual. Last year he remembered that his mom had put the gifts under the tree right after Thanksgiving and let him open one before Christmas Day. There would be at least five or six boxes would be laying there, wrapped in really inviting shiny colorful papers, but now there were none.

Frank and his mom were in the TV room. This was their typical evening ritual: His mom was watching *Jeopardy*, as she usually did after dinner, and Frank was reading his science journal. The article he was looking at was about something very interesting called "Radioactive elements." It was already difficult to understand, and he also wasn't able focus on what he was reading.

"Mom..." Frank couldn't hide his frustration in his voice. "... are we celebrating Christmas this year?" He raised his head from behind the journal and looked at his mom sitting on the couch.

His mom paused the show on TV, clearly taken by surprise, "Of course, honey, of course we will," she said. While putting the remote on the coffee table, she called Frank. "Come here." She kindly patted the couch next to her. Frank approached to take the seat. She hugged him tight and kissed him on the forehead, like she always did. Squeezing both his cheeks in her hands, she looked him in the eye and said, "Where did this come from?" Before Frank said anything, she realized what the problem was. She could see the Christmas tree right around the corner. "Oh Frankie, we have been so busy that we didn't have time to put the gifts there yet. Was that what you were worried about?" He nodded. She wrapped her arms around him again, this time more firmly. "Oh honey, don't you worry, I already got something you will really like!"

Frank's eyes widely opened with joy. "Really? Is it the mineral growing kit that I always wanted? Or the blue star bike? Oh, oh…Or is it the bike?! Or it is a telescope, isn't it?! Which one is it?"

"Well, you will have to wait one more week."

Frank dreamt about what he was going to do with his new telescope. They must have gotten a telescope for him, for sure, because he had been wanting it for the last two Christmases and they kept telling him he wasn't old enough to use it, whatever that meant. Well, he was almost twelve now, so he must be old enough. He knew that Mozart made songs when he was five. And one of his heroes, Pascal, wrote mathematical equations when he was twelve. So, Frank thought it was about the right time his parents got him a telescope.

When it was time for bed, he couldn't fall asleep. He was lying on his bed looking at different kinds of telescopes on his tablet. He wished he could buy the Hubble Telescope, which had been in space since 1990, taking amazing pictures of the universe, but he assumed it would be too expensive for his parents to buy. He saw some really good quality ones online and bookmarked his favorites. If he didn't like the one that his parents got, he was going to exchange it for one of those he liked online. This bright red medium size telescope that he found was not so expensive, because the price tag didn't have three digits.

It would be so cool to see some real stars.

He thought if he could take pictures of those stars, then he would make posters and hang them on his wall, too. He would sign the date and coordinates so that he would remember. The more he thought about this, the more excited he got. But when he tried to open a different tab suddenly the tablet said it wasn't connected to internet.

"What? What's going on?" he said. He got up from his bed and checked his desktop computer. Nope. It wasn't connected to Internet, either. *Oh no!* he thought, that meant he had to go all the way down to the basement and reset the Wi-Fi. This would happen once in a while, and each time it happened, either Frank or his dad would go downstairs turn the modem and router off and back on. Then, it would magically work again.

Good, then I can get some apple juice on my way back up, he thought. This was his motivational method that his mom thought him. Whenever he had to do something that he didn't like, as a prize, he would do something that he would actually enjoy doing once he completed the boring task.

The basement was more like an entertainment room. When his parents' best friends, Mr. and Mrs. Milton came over, they would usually hang out here. A huge TV was standing in the middle of the room, and right across that there was an extra-large cappuccino color leather couch. In the east corner there was this dark brown, wooden storage tower with shelves full of board games. Baseball posters, family pictures, awards, certificates and diplomas hung on the wall were making it hard to see what the actual wallpaper looked like. It was as if all the important but dysfunctional objects in the house were nicely dumped here. There was also a small kitchen with minibar but Frank didn't know much about it as only adults were allowed to enter.

When Frank opened the basement door, he heard someone downstairs. Actually, he heard more than one person talking. He slowly took the steps downstairs. Now he could hear more clearly. It was his mom and dad talking. But *why are they almost whispering?* he thought.

"What do you mean we don't have money?" his dad asked, sounding upset.

"What part of 'we are broke' don't you understand?" His mom sounded furious. "Do you think I enjoy this? I told Frank today that we already got his present. I lied to him – do you know how that made me feel?" She didn't look at his father but stared at a wall with her hands covering her face. Just after she started crying and sobbing, his father hugged her from behind and breathed quietly, shallowly.

"Maybe we should have never adopted him," he said.

His mom suddenly turned and looked at her husband, she looked so mad that Frank thought she was going to hit him. "Joe, what are you talking about?"

"Darling, look at us. We can't even take care of ourselves. Maybe we shouldn't have adopted him in the first place!"

Frank was confused. He didn't understand who they were talking about. Had they adopted a stray cat? But where was it? He would have seen him if they did. Oh wait…Was that what they got for him for Christmas since they couldn't buy any presents?

That's OK, Frank thought. Frank had always loved animals. He had waited for a telescope for two years; he could wait one more year.

But then his mother's words made him freeze.

"Don't you ever say that again. We adopted Frank because we wanted a child, and we committed ourselves. We knew there would be bad days as well as good days. People just don't give up on their child just like that!"

Frank felt as if the ground was pulled from under his feet. Not knowing what to do next, he quickly sat down on the steps. He was speechless. Suddenly, his thoughts had gone blank.

"Francine…I'm sorry…You misunderstood me. I'm just miserable. I have never been without a job this long in my entire life. I feel like I cannot provide for my family. I cannot even buy a gift for my son for Christmas for God's sake!"

Before Francine responded to Joe, Frank had already left the basement. He ran upstairs, shut his door. Not knowing what to think, he went back and forth in his room, trying to comprehend what he just heard. He got into his Aurora Shell, he closed the wide white doors, he pushed the red button of his LED light. He curled up in the corner and cried. He was thinking about it so much that his brain hurt. He couldn't believe that his parents – well, adoptive parents – had lied to him his whole life. Maybe they heard him, and they wanted to make a bad joke? But they seemed too serious. He just needed more proof of what he had just heard.

He came up with a brilliant idea and grabbed his tablet from the floor and started browsing their family pictures. When his mom gave this tablet to him a few years ago, she had left it up to him if he wanted to keep the albums there or not. Frank never minded them as he always had enough space on his cloud anyways. Probably this was the first time he was looking at these photos since he got the tablet. This album was from Thanksgiving, four years ago. It was a huge family reunion of both his mother's side and his father's side. Uncle Dave, Aunt Patricia, and their twins Laura and Kim were smiling by the barbecue. All had black hair. The next photo was in a house, everyone was raising their drinks to say cheers. All Frank's uncles and aunts, except Aunt Melina, were in the photo. All brown and black hair. His uncle Bobby's wife had blonde hair. *Wow*, Frank thought, *that hair is huge!* It reminded him of lion's mane. He couldn't tell his grandparents' hair color since they were grayed out already. But he knew that there was this old photo album that his mom kept on social media. He tried to check, but the Wi-Fi was still out. Then he remembered there was a single photo from his mom's graduation in the albums somewhere. He looked for this photo for almost fifteen minutes and finally found it. His Grandma Sally had light brown hair, whereas his Grandpa John had dark brown hair. *Now it makes sense*, he thought to himself, *there is no one else with red hair in the family, I'm the only one.* Then he looked at their family photo, Francine with a blue turtle neck sweater on had her arms around 8-year-old Frank, and his father Joe was smiling while his hands were both gently holding Frank's and Francine's shoulders. He didn't look like any of them. None of them were wearing glasses, either.

"I'm really adopted!" he whispered to himself in terror. He threw the tablet against the wall, curled up, rested his head on his knees and cried more. He could feel the saltiness of his tears in his mouth.

When he ran out of tears, he didn't know how long he had cried for. Maybe just a few minutes? Maybe an hour? He opened his eyes with sudden realization. *Oh no! My tablet,* he thought. Worried that he had broken his one and only true friend, he rushed to check it nervously, but thank God it was fine. "Phew!" he said, feeling lucky it wasn't damaged. Then he checked the wall to see if there was any damage and he saw that the tablet had made a hole in his favorite poster.

"Great! Today couldn't have gotten any better!"

He grabbed a roll of tape from his desk and carefully took down his poster. He laid it on the floor and carefully taped the tear back together. He was about to put the poster back on the wall but then realized the tablet had also made an even bigger hole in the wallpaper! He already hated this floral wallpaper, and now it looked even uglier.

Suddenly, it struck him. *Wait a minute...If there is a wall behind this, there shouldn't be any tears or holes in paper.*

He slowly approached the wall and had a peek inside the hole. It was pitch black, and when he brought his face closer to the hole, he could feel the cold air coming out. He peeled down a little piece of the wallpaper. It was still black. He peeled down more. That was the moment he realized there was an empty space behind the paper. *Wow!* he thought to himself, *I have found a new hiding place! This must have been an old fire place or something!*

He peeled down the wallpaper in a circular shape, just big enough that he could fit in. He was also checking to see if his mom and dad were coming upstairs because he didn't want them to see this place.

Many thoughts were crossing his mind at the same time.

Should I go in and see? But it is too dark... Oh well, I guess have to find out.

His new discovery made him so excited that he had already forgotten about the frustration his parents caused. Pulling himself up, he entered the cold and dark hole. As he kept crawling in for a few feet, inside the tunnel got colder and darker. Under his palms he could feel ice cold and soft rock. It almost felt polished so that while he was crawling, his knees were not hitting any sharp edges. *What type of rock is this?* He thought. *Volcanic? Limestone? Granite?* After a couple of feet more, the narrow tunnel took a left turn where the air felt thicker. Frank looked back, still could see his Aurora lights lightening up the entrance of the tunnel.

So cool! he thought, *I have found a secret tunnel!*

After a few seconds of crawling in the dark, he hit a wall. It was a dead end. He put his ear to the wall and tried to hear something. He wanted to know if this was their living room wall or bathroom wall or what. He thought he heard a cat meowing and scratching on the wall. This was confusing…Had his parents really gotten a cat? And which room was this?

"Frankie! Where are you?" his mom's voice echoed from the end of the tunnel.

Thinking that she was going to find out about his secret, he quickly crawled back into his Aurora Shell and taped his poster back on the wall to cover the big hole he had just opened. When his mom knocked on the door, he was putting the last piece of tape on the poster.

She opened the door slowly, "Frankie? Are you here?"

He got out of the closet with a big fake smile. "Yeah, I'm here." He was terrible at faking. His mom would always know when he was hiding something. He had always been a terrible liar, too.

He adjusted his glasses, which were falling off of his nose, and said, "Wi-Fi isn't working."

His mom sat on Frank's bed, "Oh yes. Your father is working on it." She looked around the room then said, "You are an exceptionally tidy boy, Frankie. I'm so lucky!" and smiled at Frank, "I was going to go get groceries. Do you want to come with me? Maybe we could get some ice cream on the way back?"

Francine knew that Frank would always say yes to ice-cream. So, if he said no, she would suspect something. "Of course! Cookies and cream and chocolate chip?"

"Cookies and cream and chocolate chip, as always," Francine replied. "Come on let's go."

On their way to the grocery store in the car, the only thing Frank could think of was his secret tunnel and the mysterious cat. He couldn't wait to get home and go back into that tunnel again.

"Mom?" Frank looked at her mom from the rear mirror.

"Yes darling?"

"Are we going to have a cat one day?" Frank asked. He was so curious about what his mom would say. Was she going to admit that they were hiding a cat in the house? Or maybe she would act like she didn't know anything.

His mom laughed. "Oh why? I thought you liked dogs. What were you going to name your dog again?"

"Newton, named after the scientist Isaac Newton."

"Of course," Francine nodded. She looked at him in the mirror and smiled. "No hon, unfortunately we cannot get a cat."

"Why not?" Frank once again was puzzled.

"Because your father is deadly allergic to cats."

4

THE WORMHOLE

Two days had passed, and Frank was getting more and more curious about what was going on the other side of the tunnel. Every evening he would go in and listen but he couldn't hear the cat anymore. He also searched the whole house. There was no cat. He was almost a hundred percent sure that's what he had heard: a cat. Was he going crazy?

That evening, he decided to do something different. He was going to make a sound and see if the cat on the other side responded. If the cat communicated with him, he would know that he wasn't crazy.

His mom came to his room and tucked him in, as she always did. "You have been quiet lately Frankie," she asked with worry. "Is there something wrong?"

How come my mom can tell every time something is wrong? thought Frank to himself. "No, everything is fine," he lied. He was still very upset with them. Why had they lied to him the whole time? Who were his real parents? Why didn't they want him?

Adults suck, he thought to himself.

"Frankie, you can always talk to me, you know that, right?" his mom said gently.

"Yeah, right," he said and turned his back. "Good night mom."

She kissed his head and pulled up his blanket to cover his shoulders, "Good night sweetie."

She got up and walked toward the door. "Do you want me to keep the door open, hon?"

When he was younger, Frank was afraid of dark. He would always ask his parents to leave the door open so that the hallway could lighten up his room a little bit. But it had been almost a year now since he had done that, and he wasn't afraid of the dark anymore. Because, he learned to question things. There was nothing in the dark to be afraid of. The monsters and ghosts were not real.

"No, could you close the door, please?" he responded.

Francine turned the lights off and closed the door gently behind her. Frank could hear her walking to her bedroom. Then, he heard her shut the bathroom door. Frank got up quickly and grabbed his flashlight, this time he wanted to have a good look inside the tunnel. Hurriedly, he put on his socks and his gray polar fleece jacket. He gently moved the poster that was covering the hole and he entered the tunnel slowly. Suddenly his flashlight started flashing like crazy and then stopped working. Completely. He thought the batteries must have died. He came back to the room and grabbed new batteries from his desk drawer. He put them in and checked. Now the flashlight was working. *Yes!* He was so curious to see what the tunnel really looked like inside. Maybe he could see some clues of who opened this tunnel here in the first place. Maybe they had carved their initials inside or drawn some pictures, like cave men did in the past. Frank loved researching cave art. Once he read about the oldest cave painting in Spain, which was almost 50,000 years old. This was before the Romans and the Egyptians, before people raised animals and built farms. They were still living in caves. Like Frank was hanging posters on his wall, they were painting whatever they liked on the walls. Making their living space more personal and maybe more fun.

He gently lifted the poster from its corner and he suddenly thought he heard footsteps. He froze for a second and listened... There was nothing outside Aurora Shell. He must have heard something else. He turned on his flashlight again and he started crawling into the tunnel.

But the same thing happened. He was so annoyed, as the flashlight went crazy and after flashing many times it went off again. But then he realized it wasn't about the batteries. "It is this place..." Frank whispered in surprise. This place was not letting him use his flashlight. *Bummer!* he thought and left his flashlight in Aurora Shell. He started crawling into the dark again. After a good thirty seconds of crawling, he took the left turn. It was getting colder and colder. He thought maybe he was getting closer to the outside door, and that was why it was getting colder. Maybe?

He was finally at the end of the tunnel, but he hesitated. What if his parents heard him instead of the cat? How was he going to explain this?

Finally, he knocked on the wall, three times: *Knock... Knock...Knock...*

Then he put his ear back to the wall and listened. No sound. Silence.

He knocked again, three times: *Knock...Knock...Knock...*

Then something unexpected happened. Someone knocked back, three times. *Knock...Knock...Knock...*

Frank could hear his heartbeat. What if it was his mom? If she realized that it was him, he worried that she would never let him use the tunnel again. Once, he remembered, when they were playing at Ramzi's house, they had crawled in the AC unit like in the movies. After his mom heard about this, she didn't allow him to do that again saying that vents were dangerous. He didn't want to lose this secret place, though! So, he kept quiet.

Then something strange happened. Frank heard the same scratching noise: The cat! The cat was here! He wasn't crazy. He could hear the cat meowing.

"Hello?" said a sudden voice.

Frank was frozen.

This voice didn't sound like anybody he knew. First of all, he sounded young, like Frank's age. Then, this couldn't be their neighbor next door, because they didn't have young children. Their daughter was going to college and their son was married and besides, he lived somewhere else.

Frank was scared but also it was a relief that it wasn't his mom on the other side. He felt the courage to answer.

"Hello?"

There was a long silence. No cat sounds, either.

"Who are you?" the boy asked from the other side. He sounded scared.

"I'm Frank."

"What are you doing in the wall Frank?" said the boy. This was a very good question and Frank didn't know how to answer it.

"Umm…I found a tunnel in my room, and at the end of the tunnel I ended up here," said Frank, frankly.

"Cool! I love tunnels!" the boy said excitedly.

"What is your name?" Frank asked.

"My name is Andy. Are you our neighbor's kid? My mom said our neighbor has a son who likes climbing up the walls and hiding. She told me not to hang out with him."

"I don't think we are neighbors, actually," Frank replied, confused.

"Oh…that's weird." Andy sounded confused, too. "Anyway, I gotta go to school now. Talk to you later, wall boy!"

"My name is Frank!"

Frank didn't like to be called other names rather than his name. This kid in school used to call him "Frankoogle" because Frank would Google everything. This other kid called him "stalker" just because they happened to be in the same places that day by coincidence. But then the name stuck.

All of a sudden, he realized that it was almost midnight. What school could Andy be going to this late?

"Hey Andy! What's your school?" Frank yelled.

No response. Andy had left already.

Frank crawled back into his room, covered the hole back up with the poster, carefully taped. Then he opened his bedroom door slowly to check the hallway. His floor was dark and quiet except for his dad snoring and the clock on the wall ticking. The clock said 11:22 PM. He closed his door gently. He took off his jacket and socks then lay in his bed. He started thinking about Andy. Who was he, and how come his parents let him leave home this late? And the bigger question was…Where was he? He didn't live next door and definitely didn't live in Frank's house. This was so confusing and fascinating at the same time.

Frank barely slept that night.

The next day was Saturday. Frank loved Saturdays because it was pancake day. He could eat as many pancakes as he wanted, and he would get to sit down with both his parents at breakfast. But this Saturday was different. He was not excited to share time with his parents anymore. They weren't even his real parents. To him, they were liars. Also, pancakes weren't as exciting anymore since the only thing he could think of now was his new potential friend, Andy.

"Would you like some eggs too, hon?" said Francine.

"No, thanks," Frank answered.

Both Francine and Joe laughed. Frank raised his eyebrows, "What? What are you laughing at?"

"I was actually asking your dad, but it is good to know that you don't want eggs, Frankie," said Francine.

"Oh…" said Frank.

"No thanks, I'm good," Joe replied. "I have a job interview on Monday," he said proudly, checking both Francine's and Frank's reactions.

Francine left the pancake batter on the counter and cleaned her hands quickly with the towel to give a big hug to her husband. "I'm so happy to hear that darling," she said joyfully, "I'm sure you will do great!"

Frank was quiet. Having noticed that, Joe asked, "Hey Frankie, aren't you happy to hear what I just said?"

Frank looked at him, not even trying to smile, he said, "Yes, I'm…Does this mean you will have a job soon?"

"Probably," Joe answered. "It depends on how the interview goes on Monday." He swallowed a big piece of pancake.

"Do people lie during interviews?" Frank asked all of a sudden. This question created an awkward silence.

Joe and Francine looked at each other, surprised by the nature of the question.

Joe waited till he finished the food in his mouth. He cleaned his mouth with the napkin and turned to Frank. "I'm sure some people lie. But that is not good, you know. Nobody likes liars because you can't trust them. They won't give you the job if they think you are not reliable," he said.

"Hmm, I see…" Frank replied, looking at his pancake.

Francine and Joe looked at each other again. They both knew something was up with Frank. Francine couldn't help but said, "Is there anything you want to tell us, hon?"

Frank took a bite of his pancake. "No, not really."

He was angry that they had both lied to him and yet they kept saying lying was bad. He still wanted them to be happy though, because they were good to him most of the time. "Good luck with the interview Dad," he said.

"Thanks kiddo!" replied his father, ruffling Frank's hair.

Frank spent the whole day waiting for the night to come so that he could go into the tunnel again and talk to Andy. Frank and his family were invited to a barbecue party next door, and they spent hours there eating, drinking and talking. It was an exceptionally warm and sunny day for December. The house had a huge open living room with big windows. Frank's favorite part of this room were the white puffy couches and sofas. They reminded him of clouds. Plus, they were perfect for reading. Frank was reading his book in the corner of this cloud couch when one of the neighbor's kids came and asked him if he wanted to play. This book about earthquakes and volcanoes was one of his favorites. Its encyclopedia-like shiny thick pages had full-page high-resolution photos. It still had that ink smell which Frank always liked. His book was so interesting that he didn't want to go play a stupid game and waste his time.

Frank said, "I think I'm OK, thanks."

"Well, are you sure? We need one more person on our team for the water fight. Andy brought these cool water guns. Do you want to join?"

Frank never enjoyed water fights. He saw them as a waste of time. Besides, wet clothes always made him uncomfortable. It's winter for God's sake. He was pretty sure his mom wouldn't like that, either. But he heard the name "Andy" and thought, *Is that him?! Maybe he IS a neighbor boy!*

Frank left his book on the seat. "Sure, sounds fun!" he said and followed the kid to the backyard. There were around ten or eleven kids there, filling their toy guns and balloons with water. Frank nervously checked everyone's faces. Was that him? The one with the glasses? Or maybe the blond guy next to him? But he didn't look younger than 9th grade.

"Hey!" the kid yelled at Frank. "Are you coming or what?"

Frank quickly walked towards the group, cleared his throat and asked, "Umm…Which one of you is Andy?"

"What?" the kid couldn't hear him well.

Frank raised his voice a little bit more. "Which one of you is Andy?"

"Oh!" the kid turned to this huge guy in the corner, "Hey Andy!"

Andy, with his red hair and freckles all over his face, somewhat looked like Frank. But he was way taller and chubbier which was not what Frank had pictured in his mind.

"Hey Arnold!" he yelled back. "Are you guys in?"

Frank didn't think this was his new friend's voice. But how could he be sure? It was such a short conversation. Definitely, Frank had to make sure. So, he yelled back, "Hey Andy, this is Frank! The wall boy!" Andy looked at him as if Frank was the weirdest kid on earth. He shook his head and continued filling his balloon with water. Frank was now sure that this was not the same Andy. Andy would have recognized him once he heard Frank's nickname.

All their neighbors were at this party. Now, he was more certain than ever that Andy was not a neighbor boy.

Frank didn't want to play. He went back to the couch to finish his book. Seeing his son coming back, his mom left her group of friends in the kitchen and approached him. "Hey there!"

"Hey," Frank said.

"For a second you looked like you were going to have some fun with those kids. But then you changed your mind and came back to read?" she said.

"Yeah, I guess…" He raised his eyes from his book and looked at his mom. "It's just…The book seemed more interesting than their game," he shrugged.

"Oh, honey. I just want you to make friends and have fun." Francine said.

"Don't worry Mom. I will." He smiled. Of course, he would; he had meant Andy.

Frank went to bed at around 9:30 that night. While his mom was tucking him in, she said, "You are going to bed pretty early, hon, are you feeling sick? Did you get wet on that water fight or something?" She placed her hand on Frank's forehead to check his temperature.

Frank said, "No, I'm feeling fine. Just tired. We were out playing all day, Mom."

"You mean *they* were out playing all day. Every time I checked, you were reading your book, Frankie. I said it before, I'm saying it again. You need to play with your friends, talk with them. I'm worried that you will feel lonely one day. We need other people in our lives to be happy."

Maybe she was right. But for now, Frank was happy with his books and the other kids were not interesting enough to talk or spend time with. "OK." he said, "I will try."

After his mom kissed him goodnight and closed his door, Frank jumped off of his bed and went straight into the tunnel. Knocked on the wall again, three times. *Come on Andy, talk to me!* Frank thought.

"Hello wall boy," came Andy's voice.

"Could you please stop calling me that?" Frank replied. "My name is Frank." Although he was mad at him, weirdly he was happy to hear Andy's voice. He thought to himself, *this is definitely not the kid I've met today. I knew it!*

"Haha," Andy said, "OK. Fine, don't get mad."

"Do you go to a night school?" Frank asked.

"Night school? What is that? Yikes! It sounds terrible. I go to school in the morning. Really early in the morning."

Frank tried to make sense of what he just heard. "But... The other day, when you said you were going to school, it was almost midnight."

"Hmm. Maybe you were still dreaming, Frank. Because it was 7 AM or so in the morning when we talked."

Weird..., Frank thought. He started to think about what could be happening here. He couldn't come up with any logical answers and it was driving him crazy.

"Frank?"

"Yeah?"

"You are still there, good. I thought you were gone for a second."

"No, I was just thinking."

"Thinking about how to cross this wall?"

"Yeah that and...About what the heck is happening here."

"I could try to take down the wall. I know where my mom keeps the tool box. I could grab a hammer and give it a try?"

Frank answered nervously, "I don't think that would be a good idea."

"Why not?" Andy sounded confused. "Don't you want to meet?"

Frank was trying to understand what was happening. Flashlight didn't work, so it could be an electromagnetic problem in this tunnel. Time zones were different, which totally didn't make sense, and Andy wasn't the neighbor boy, so who was he? Most importantly, *where* was he? "I need to do some research, Andy! But I will be back soon, I promise!" Frank said.

"Wait! Research about what?"

"Don't have time to explain! I will tell you soon enough!" Frank crawled back in his Aurora Shell and quickly grabbed his tablet. He opened the Internet browser and typed "Magnetic field change" and "tunnel" in the search bar. He excitedly skimmed over the search results. There was nothing useful. Then he typed in "Time zone change and magnetic field change." Only time zone-related info came up. He was talking to himself now, "Think Frank, think!" While his thoughts were rushing through his mind, his eye caught a glimpse of his Big Bang poster that hung on the right side of the tunnel. He typed in "Different galaxies and tunnel and magnetic field."

"Here we go!" he said. There were many results to go through. He clicked on the first one. The page opened. The headline read, "Are scientists about to discover a mirror universe?"

Of course, this article caught his attention. He continued reading curiously. The article read, "New experiments look to the interplay between neutrons and magnetic fields to observe our universal reflection, meaning *another dimension* which is the mirror image of our universe."

He dropped his tablet. His mouth was wide open with awe. He looked up to his Big Bang poster and smiled so big.

"Andy is in another dimension..." he said to himself, having a hard time believing in what he just said.

"This tunnel...This tunnel is a...A WORMHOLE!" Frank screamed, jumping up and down. Then he realized his parents were still asleep, so he covered his mouth while he was dancing in his Aurora Shell. He didn't remember when was the last time he was this excited before. "I have to go tell Andy."

He jumped in the tunnel, quickly crawled until he arrived at Andy's wall.

"Andy! Are you there? I think I have it all figured out!" said Frank.

"You sound really excited! Tell me then," said Andy, "I want to know what's going on."

"You're going to lose your mind when you hear this: This tunnel is a wormhole!"

"A wormhole? Where? In the tunnel?" Andy was grossed-out. "Yikes, are you sitting in a pile of worms?"

"No, no you don't understand. It is a passage through space and time and...And it is a shortcut to another, another...Another universe!"

Frank was ecstatic! If he could jump up and down in that tunnel, he would. This was just not a hiding place. This was a wormhole. A WORMHOLE. All his life, well for 11.5 years, he had studied space, and now he was witnessing something his friends or family or maybe another human being could never do!

After a long silence Andy said, "Sorry friend, but I don't know what you are talking about...I'm looking at my Big Bang Theory poster right now, and I see the universes but can't see any wormholes."

"Maybe you should Google it," Frank said.

"Goo- what?"

"Uhm…Google?"

"What is Google? That sounds funny. Like goggles? Hahaha!"

Frank realized that probably they had a different world out there. Started in a different time, shaped by different events and people. Maybe Google's CEO was never born in Andy's universe. This was fascinating! Then, he suddenly realized another thing.

"Hey Andy?"

"Yeah?"

"You said you were looking at a Big Bang theory poster, right? Where is it?"

"Right in front of me. I'm still looking at it, by the way. Still no wormholes. What do they look like?"

All of a sudden, it made sense for Frank. He dismissed Andy's question completely. "Hey Andy I gotta go back to my room but I will be back in a minute, don't go anywhere, OK.?"

"Again?? OK. for me but are you alright? You sound a little crazy."

While Frank crawled back to his Aurora Shell, he couldn't believe what was going on. If his theory was true, then…Then this would be the coolest thing that a kid could ever ask for!

He finally arrived at the Shell and quickly pulled the poster back to cover the hole. Frank looked at the poster in detail. It had been given to him on his 10th birthday by his science teacher Mr. Jenkins. He knew how Frank was interested in space and he also had a copy of the same poster.

Frank was trying to find a clue on the poster. He thought that he had been able to find this wormhole because of something in relation with this poster. *Where was it? Andy was right… There are no wormholes here. Come on Frank, look. Look closely, what is it?*

Wait…

Suddenly, the taped part in his poster caught his eye. The tear that he taped back together was on a galaxy among the far left of the universe, where the Big Bang started. The resolution was not perfect and Frank had no idea if there was a wormhole or not. But he came up with an idea and wanted to give a shot. He crawled back into the tunnel. When he arrived at the end he knocked and yelled, "Hey Andy, are you still there?"

"Yes, I'm here! What took you so long?"

"Listen, I have an idea. It might sound crazy, but I think it will work."

"O-kay…You're scaring me a little. But go on."

"Do you remember the tool box you were talking about? Go get it and we will hammer down the wall."

"You disappeared for fifteen minutes and came back with what you call a 'crazy idea,' and now you are telling me that I should do exactly what I already had said I would do in the first place?"

"Well, that sounds complicated. Just go get the hammer, and I will tell you about the plan."

"OK. hang on. It must be in the garage."

Frank could hear Andy running out of the room. He felt butterflies in his stomach. This was not making any sense but at the same time, it was making a lot of sense. He looked at his watch, but his watch had stopped working since he had entered the tunnel. It must have been fifteen, maybe twenty minutes or so since Andy left. "Where are you Andy?" said Frank to himself, getting impatient.

"Hey, Frank?"

"Yes! Did you get it?"

"Yeah. But I'm sure my mom will hear if the whole wall comes down."

"Don't worry, it won't be the whole wall. Wait…What is that sound? Are you eating something?"

"Oops! Yeah. My mom made chocolate chip cookies last night. Oh, they are so good. Do I make that much noise when I eat? Had no idea!"

"I was waiting for you here, Andy, you know?"

"Relax, I got some for you, too. Hahaha. So, what is next, tell me the plan."

"First, make sure your door is locked," said Frank.

"Good point!" said Andy. Frank could hear him shut the door and push the lock in. "All set!"

"Second, turn on some music," said Frank.

"What kind?" Andy said, jokingly.

"Anything that would block the sound," Frank was getting impatient again.

Andy started playing a rock song. Then Frank heard Andy turning up the volume a little. He tried to recognize the song, but he had never heard that music in his life.

"Now," said Frank nervously, "You will see this galaxy on the far-left corner of the Big Bang poster, it is bright yellow."

"Hmm…Let me see…"

"Above it there is another galaxy with bright red at the center."

"Yes! I think I've found it. Now what?"

"Hammer there. Exactly where the yellow spot is," said Frank.

"This sounds pretty crazy. You were right about that!" said Andy. "But I will do it, anyway."

BANG! That was the first blow of the hammer.

Frank was so amazed by everything that was happening that he couldn't even process the moment.

BANG!

He was talking to someone his age from another universe.

BANG!

He had found a wormhole in his closet and now he was going to actually see this person.

BANG!

His stomach started to hurt and his heart was beating fast. Then he suddenly heard the sound:

BAM!

There was a medium-size hole in the wall now. A beam of yellow light was coming into the dark tunnel. Frank was speechless. It had worked! He couldn't believe that it worked!

Frank saw two fingers entering from the hole, grabbing the wall paper.

Then he heard Andy tear the whole wallpaper down.

5

ANDY

A pair of big brown eyes were looking at Frank in shock. Andy was taller than what Frank had thought, and skinnier. He had dark brown hair and freckles. The first thing Frank noticed about Andy's room was a plate full of chocolate chip cookies on his bed.

"Hi!" said Frank.

"Hi…" answered Andy still in shock.

"Should I come in?" smiled Frank.

"Oh, I'm so sorry, let me help you," Andy gave Frank a hand, and Frank jumped from the wormhole into the room.

Frank couldn't believe his eyes. This was the exact room that his parents slept in. But it was covered with wall papers now, and the furniture was completely new. Most importantly, it was a kid's room. There were a lot of superhero posters on the wall. But they weren't Batman or Superman. One of them looked like Superman with a blue suit and red cape, but there was a giant P instead of S on his chest. Superman looked Asian, and his hair was much longer than the Superman that Frank knew. There were a lot of books on the bookshelf in the corner, which made Frank immediately excited. The carpet in the room was bright red, and it was quite dirty. The room looked like it hadn't been cleaned for a while. It was tidy but dirty.

"Cookies?" Andy asked, smiling and holding out the plate.

Frank grabbed one and had a bite. "How old are you?"

"Eleven," Andy replied.

"I will be twelve in six months," said Frank, walking and looking around curiously. He was looking at the library that Andy had and he realized he didn't know any of the books. *Law and Order for Young Adults* read one. *History of Philosophy* said another. *How to Fight Anxiety* was an interesting one. Frank thought that he would get anxious sometimes. That was why he built Aurora Shell in the first place. He would love to know more about it.

"You have a lot of books here," said Frank.

"Yeah…I like to read." Andy took another bite from his cookie and spilled more crumbs on the red carpet.

"Where is your tablet?" asked Frank.

"I don't have one. My mom said we can't afford it."

"That sucks," replied Frank. For a second, he realized he would be so bored without his tablet and his computer. He never thought he would be thankful for them. Indeed, he was!

"Who is this?" Frank pointed at the Superman-like superhero.

"Oh, the Powerman! I used to be a big fan of him, but now I think I don't believe in heroes anymore."

"Why?" Frank asked.

"I don't know. I guess I'm growing up."

"Yeah, they are pretty made up," Frank said, smiling.

"Also, if they were real, they would have done something for me already."

Frank frowned in curiosity. "What do you mean?"

Andy shook his shoulder. "Forget about it. So, tell me, who is your favorite hero?"

Frank didn't even think, "I have two: Isaac Newton and Nikola Tesla!"

"Hmm...That's weird," Andy sounded confused.

"I know, they are not 'superheroes'..." Frank did that quotation mark gesture while saying that. "But they are real life heroes, they are scientists that changed lives of millions!"

"If they are that important why don't they teach us about them in class?" Andy sat on his bed, still holding his plate of cookies.

"For sure, they do!" Frank responded with awe. Then he realized he was from a different universe. Maybe there had never been an Isaac Newton or Nikola Tesla here. "OK. Tell me some scientist names then." Frank got very excited and jumped on the bed, right next to Andy.

Andy, with the last piece of cookie in his mouth, stopped chewing for a second to think. Frank stared at him with such an amusement that Andy started to think there was something wrong with him. "Uhm..." Andy was obviously trying to think of some names from the science class. "Victor Silverman, who discovered the electricity...Patrick McCormick, who discovered Penicilliquo. Hmm, who else...Dimitri Klonoslov, the astronaut who stepped on the moon for the first time and...Leonardo Da

Vinci who performed the first heart surgery!" Andy shrugged his shoulders as if saying, "That's all I remember now."

Frank's jaw dropped. "This is fascinating!" he whispered.

"What is that? My science knowledge? Hahaha, I wouldn't use those words exactly, but–"

"No, no, no, you don't understand Andy. We belong to two different universes. That's why we have different heroes, different histories and so different scientists, politicians, inventors, and artists!"

"Hahaha! That's so funny!" Andy suddenly stopped laughing when he realized Frank was serious. "Wait…You are serious."

Frank nodded.

"No way." Andy stood up. "OK. In the beginning, I thought you were a little weird but what you are saying makes you a total cray cray!"

Before Frank got the chance to explain his point, a woman with a hoarse voice yelled from downstairs.

"Where are you, you little bastard?! Turn off that music!"

Frank could see the sudden panic in Andy's eyes. Andy was absolutely terrified. "Oh no, we must have made too much noise. She woke up. Before she sees you, you gotta go."

"Tomorrow," said Frank. "Tomorrow I will show you my side. Then, you will see that I'm not crazy."

"Bring your lazy ass down here and make me some dinner!" said the angry woman's voice, followed by a long nasty cough.

"Fine," replied Andy to Frank. "Now, please go!"

Frank climbed into the wormhole, but before he left, he turned back and asked, "Who is that woman yelling at you? She sounds mad."

"My mom," Andy replied.

Frank saw that fear again in Andy's eyes.

"See you tomorrow, Frank," said Andy and then quickly covered the hole back with the poster.

6

HELLO, THE OTHER SIDE!

On his way back to his room through the wormhole, Frank thought about how fascinating it was to experience two different worlds with their similarities and differences.

Suddenly he stopped crawling. The questions in his mind were overpowering. "Is Andy's country even called the United States? Who is the president? Did World War I or World War II happen at all?" Then he paused. "And what the heck is Penicilliquo?" He had so many questions. He kept on crawling and when he finally got back to his Aurora Shell, he thought about his new friend. Frank really liked him. But his mom was scary.

Why is she so mean to him? Andy seemed like a nice person. Why would someone get angry with such a nice person? Frank wondered.

He quickly covered the hole with his Big Bang poster and suddenly heard a noise. *Oh no, I must have stayed on the Andy's side too long,* he thought, *my parents must be up! What if they realized that I was gone and they called the police?!* Frank quickly tiptoed back to his bed and slowly pulled his blanket over his chest. He couldn't hear anything; the noise was gone. Just to make sure, he got up and checked outside his door, but he couldn't see any shadows moving. Then his eyes caught the time on the clock across the hallway. It was still showing the time that he had left to go to Andy's place.

That's impossible!! Frank thought, *I spent almost an hour there!*

He was so confused again. He sat in the bed for a while trying to understand how this was possible. This was another mystery for him to solve. Just before he fell asleep, he thought about Andy's angry mother again.

I hope he is OK, he thought, just a few seconds before he fell asleep.

The next day, Frank was super excited about showing Andy "his side" which would be "the other side" for him. His parents had to leave Frank alone for two hours that day, because his mom had to work and his dad had a job interview downtown.

"I'm a grown-up now," Frank told his mom. "I don't need a babysitter. Don't worry, I will be fine!" Besides, this wasn't the first time he had stayed home alone, anyway. He had actually barely felt that he was alone the last time, since he was on his tablet all day long.

"I will see you in a couple of hours, hon," said Francine and gave Frank a kiss on his forehead.

"See you mom," said Frank, trying to hide his excitement.

After he shut and locked the door, he ran to the kitchen and peeked from the window, watching his mom leaving the garage with their pick-up. After he made sure that his mom had gone far enough, he quickly ran upstairs. First, he checked the time, it was 10:13 AM. He got into his Aurora Shell, carefully removed the Big Bang poster and crawled into the wormhole.

When he reached the end, he sat down and whispered cautiously, "Andy! Hey Andy, are you there?"

No response.

Ugh…We should have agreed on a certain time! Frank thought, regretfully. After sitting there for five minutes, Frank decided to go in and find Andy.

He carefully pushed the corner of the poster out from where it was taped. He started to peel it off and finally he was able to open his way entirely. He jumped into the room. The bed was unmade, and the room looked as dirty as yesterday. He tiptoed to the door and opened it slowly. The door opened to a long hallway. This was Frank's hallway! But it looked older and darker. The dark brown floral wallpapers smelled like cigarettes, and they were peeled off in places, revealing the dark brown wood underneath. Because Frank was familiar with the layout, he decided to check what his room looked like in Andy's world. He tiptoed toward his room. The wood under his feet was squeaky, and he didn't want to get Andy in trouble, so he was really trying to be quiet, like a thief.

Finally, he was there, right in front of his door. He slowly turned the golden door knob. The door opened with a light squeak. *Everything is squeaky in this house!* Frank thought with panic. His room was dark like any other place in this house. He walked inside carefully to better see what was inside. The curtains were so dusty that their color had turned smoky grey. The carpet looked like as if it hadn't been vacuumed for years. There were only a few things in this room. There was a wooden desk with some books and toys on them. They looked old and dusty. Some of them even had spider webs on them. Then there was a book shelf in the corner of the room. Frank got closer to see what kind of books they were; maybe he could borrow one or two… Or three. They were really colorful and had lots of drawings in them. *They must be for little kids*, Frank thought, *maybe they used to be Andy's?*

When he was getting ready to leave the room, something caught his eye by the wall. When he got closer, he saw a cradle. Something engraved in the headboard caught his attention. By wiping off the dust on what it looked like letters with the back of his hand he revealed the word *Mike*.

"What are you doing here?"

Frank heard Andy's voice just behind him. He turned and saw Andy standing in the shadows, at the door, looking worried.

"I came here to find you, I thought I could show you the other side today," Frank replied.

"You cannot just enter my home and walk around like that!" Andy was trying to whisper but was clearly upset.

"I'm sorry, I really am sorry, I just wanted to –"

"Let's go to my room before my mom sees us, come on, quick!"

The two tiptoed back to Andy's room. On the way, Frank saw one of the rooms at the end of the hallway. This was a guest room in Frank's house. The door was ajar, and he could see someone on a sofa, back turned against the door. He knew there was someone because he could see a hand hanging from the arm of the sofa, holding a smoking cigarette. When he and Andy got into the room and closed the door, Frank heard a very strong and long cough.

"Is that your mom?" Frank asked.

"Yes," Andy replied, "She smokes a lot."

Andy made sure the door was locked. Then he looked at Frank and smiled, "OK. I'm ready now. Show me that you are not crazy."

Suddenly they were both startled by the same sound.

"Meow."

Now something was scratching the door.

"Oh, Love!" Andy said.

"Who?" Frank asked, confused.

Andy opened the door and this fluffy, smoky light gray cat ran into the room and started rubbing against Frank's legs. When the cat raised its head and looked directly into Frank's eyes, he saw its beautiful light green eyes. Frank had seen the cat the day before but had never paid attention to its eyes.

"She likes you," said Andy and grabbed the cat.

"Did you name her Love? Never heard of someone naming their cat like that."

"Yes, I named her Love." Andy was petting Love, kissing her, and she was purring back. "That is the only way I can hear a nice word from my mom, when she calls the cat by her name." Andy smiled right after saying these words but it wasn't that funny for Frank. Actually, Frank felt really sad all of a sudden.

"Come on, we don't have much time, I don't want her to notice that I'm gone," said Andy.

"Alrighty, let's do it!" replied Frank with joy, his excitement was back.

First, Frank climbed up to the wormhole and then he helped Andy and Love to come up. Suddenly, Love started hissing and making some nervous sounds.

"Come on, Love, it is going to be fun!" said Andy. "There is nothing to be scared of, I'm right here."

But then the strangest thing happened.

As Andy entered the wormhole, he felt the weight disappear from under his arm. Andy shouted, "Where is Love? She was right here!"

Frank was puzzled. "Are you sure she didn't run back?"

"No way, she was right here in my arms! I will go back and check," said Andy.

When he looked into the room, he saw Love by the entrance. He grabbed her and when he tried to take her in the wormhole, she disappeared again. When he pulled his hands out of the hole, Love was in his hands, alive and well. "I can't believe this!" Andy whispered to himself.

"Hey! What's taking you so long?" Frank asked.

Andy put Love on the ground and petted her. "Good girl, you stay here, I will be back soon!"

When he crawled back next to Frank, he looked at him and said, "You are not crazy, my friend. There is really something weird going on here."

"Where is Love?" asked Frank.

Andy, still in shock, said, "I...I guess she doesn't exist outside my universe."

They looked at each other with amusement. "Well, that's good news I guess, I just learned that my dad is allergic to cats," said Frank, "He could have noticed her. It is good not to take any risks. Don't worry, she will be OK."

When they arrived at Frank's Aurora Shell, Andy was speechless with amusement. He yelled, "Wow! This place is super cool!"

He started looking around, he looked at Frank's magazines on the floor and the solar system hanging from the ceiling. He touched each and every planet. Frank had to leave Andy alone in Aurora Shell because wanted to check the time to see if what had happened yesterday would happen again. It was still 10:13 AM.

"Wow, unbelievable!" he said. He ran back into his closet to find Andy. He couldn't wait till he told him about what he just found out. When Frank went through his clothes and finally reached his Shell, Andy seemed super interested in his *Star Wars* action figures.

"What is this team? Are they superheroes?" asked Andy, holding R2-D2 toy in his one hand and Yoda in the other.

"Umm...Not really," Frank said, "They are from a book, or a movie, or both, I guess. It is called *Star Wars*." Frank sat next to Andy and grabbed the Darth Vader action figure. "Maybe we can watch that movie together one day?"

Andy was superexcited about this idea. "Really? I would love that!"

Frank said, "Yeah, I watched each movie like ten times already, but, we can." He left the Darth Vader figurine on the floor, "But now, we have a more interesting and exciting thing going on!" Frank couldn't hide his excitement.

"What is it?"

"When I leave this universe to visit your universe, time stops here, in my universe. When I came to get you, it was 10:13 AM, when we got back it was still 10:13 AM. Isn't that awesome?!"

"Hmm…" Andy looked puzzled. Then suddenly he jumped with joy, "Does this mean that now that I'm here, the time has stopped in my universe, too?"

"Probably…" Frank shrugged. "I guess we will figure it out."

"Yay! That means I can stay here as long as I want to!"

"Well, you can stay here as long as my parents are not here."

They both got out of Aurora Shell. The gray clouds were hiding the morning sun and the shadow of the rustling tree branches were dancing on Frank's carpet. The wind sounded cold, but this newborn friendship had warmed up the room already.

"I've searched for the word Penicilliquo, by the way," Frank said.

"Oh, you could have asked me!" Andy said, looking around the room.

"It is called Penicillin in our universe. It cures infections. Named after Penicillium molds by its discoverer Scottish scientist Alexander Fleming. But I guess in your universe it is named as Penicilliquo because it was discovered by someone else..."

"Patrick McCormick." Andy was all ears now.

"Yes! I looked at the meaning of *liquo* in Latin and it meant *filtered*. So, I guess Mr. McCormick named his discovery by following this logic. I don't know. I just find these things fascinating. Don't you think?"

"Sure, they are." Andy nodded. "Huh…Who would have thought?" he said while walking around Frank's room. "What is *quantum theory?*" He held up a yellow book.

"Ah, that's my book. I don't understand it yet, but it is quite interesting. I own it now but I will read it in three years or so, when I understand physics better."

"Hahaha, you are weird and funny Frank, I like you." While putting the book back on the shelf. "So, you like physics?"

"I do, yes. It is everywhere we look. But not everybody sees what I see."

"Show me!" said Andy, "I want to see!"

Frank was surprised. He was not expecting Andy to take him seriously. Because no one took him seriously when he talked about science. They always thought that Frank was nerdy and boring. Finally, someone was interested in his world. This excited Frank very much.

"OK. Sit." Frank showed Andy his turning chair. Andy looked at Frank for a second, not sure what was happening, but then he followed.

After sitting, "Now what?" he asked.

"Open your arms and legs," Frank said, "as if you are jumping."

Andy did exactly what Frank said. He opened his arms wide, as if he was asking for a big hug. Then, he stretched his legs open as if he was ready to fly.

"Let's do it!" Andy said.

Frank suddenly started spinning the chair very fast.

"Hahaha, this is so much fun!" Andy laughed.

A few seconds later Frank ordered, "Now shrink, I mean put your arms and legs together, in the middle of the chair."

Andy followed Frank's order and suddenly started spinning even faster. "Woohoohoo! The room is spinning so fast! Hahaha! Love physics!"

Andy was laughing and cheering at the same time. After Frank stopped the chair from moving, the room was still spinning for Andy. "Wow, this was fun. Oh wait…The world is spinning, hahaha!" He closed his eyes so that the world could stop rotating, but he still felt disoriented it in his head.

"So, what was all that?" asked Andy. His eyes were still closed.

"Well," said Frank pushing up the bridge of his sliding glasses, "It is called momentum. Momentum increases with either the speed or the size of the object. So, I pushed you with the same speed at both times, but when you shrank, your size got smaller, in order to keep the momentum same, your speed increased. Get it?"

"Wow," said Andy, with excitement. "But no. I didn't get it."

They both laughed.

"I didn't understand, but I liked it," said Andy. Suddenly, he was distracted by what he saw. "Oh! Is that snow?" Andy ran to the window and looked outside in amazement. It had been snowing since morning, leaving the neighborhood under a white blanket. "This is the first time I've seen snow! Except for the movies and TV shows, of course," said Andy. "Really? Seasons must be different then in your city. It always snows here in winter."

"They say that it used to snow before," replied Andy sadly, "But then it started to get warmer every year, and we stopped getting any snow." Andy sighed. "So unfortunate...Look at this! I mean, this is beautiful!" Andy put both of his hands on the cold glass window leaving his hand prints. "I would love to open the window and touch the snow but I don't want the cold get into your room."

"Well, technically the warm air leaves the room and moves into a colder area, which is, in this example, outside," said Frank quietly then fixed his glasses again.

"What did you say?" Andy asked, still looking outside.

In that moment, Frank realized that this was why he never had good friendships. Because he kept correcting others. He didn't want to lose Andy, no, not this time. So, he kept his thoughts to himself.

"Nothing!" he said, "Maybe it's not a good idea to open the window. But I was going to ask you if you want to go outside and check out the snow? I can lend you a sweater and a coat, if you like."

"REALLY?" Andy's eyes were popping out. He jumped up and down and gave a big hug to Frank. Because Frank was way smaller than him, when they hugged, he realized Frank's feet weren't touching the ground anymore.

"You're welcome. But we don't have much time. We have to keep moving!" Frank said.

They went downstairs and Frank ran to the fridge, got a cinnamon cookie for himself and got one for Andy.

"Here you go!" Frank said, "My mom made those yesterday."

"Thank you!" Andy replied while trying to get into the winter coat, "This is a little tight for me, but I think it will work."

Andy put on Frank's black hat, black gloves and bright orange color coat. The coat didn't cover Andy's belly or wrists, but he was able to zip it all the way up.

"We are all set!" said Frank.

Andy clapped his hands and jumped up and down with excitement.

"Are you always excited about things like this?" Frank asked. It seemed like everything was amusing to his new friend.

"Yes, why not?" Andy answered, "What is wrong with being excited about things?"

"Nothing!" Frank shrugged, "I guess, I have never met anyone like you," he smiled, "Go ahead, open the door!"

When Andy opened the front door, he could not believe his eyes. It was as if he was watching a magic trick. He had seen rain before but this was much more fun to watch. "It is so quiet out here!" Andy said in amazement. "When it rains, it is so loud. But this is very peaceful."

Frank had never heard someone his age used the word "peaceful". He was right though…For some reason, it did feel very peaceful.

Andy slowly stepped in the snow and sank an inch or so. "Wow!" he said, looking at his shoes, "Look, I can leave my footprints!"

Suddenly Frank realized that this wasn't going to do any good because his mom was going to be back in an hour and she could see those foot prints. She didn't like when Frank played outside when he was home alone.

"Let's roll in the snow!" said Frank, proud to find a smart and fun solution to the problem.

"What? That's crazy!" said Andy laughing.

Frank lay down in the snow and started rolling back and forth like a rolling pin. *Brrr! It is so cold!* he thought to himself. Quickly Andy followed him and soon they were both rolling and laughing in the snow.

"We don't have to make a snowman," said Andy.

"Why?"

"We already have two, look at us!" they both laughed. Yet Frank was once more amazed by the fact that how Andy was finding everything fascinating and almost everything was making him happy.

They threw snowballs at each other, they tried to build a castle, but it was taking too much time.

"I'm afraid we have to go back in," said Frank, "My mom will be here any minute."

"Oh, OK." replied Andy, sounding disappointed, cleaning the snow stuck on his gloves.

When they got back in the house, the tree in the living room corner caught Andy's eyes.

"I don't even remember the last Christmas I had with mom," said sadly.

"What would you wish for Christmas?" Frank asked to cheer up his friend.

Without even thinking, Andy responded, "Snow would be nice!"

"You can't gift wrap snow though," Frank laughed.

"Yeah, I guess that would be a very messy gift!" Andy laughed back.

While they were laughing, Frank noticed two headlights in the distance, approaching fast. This was his mom's pickup. "Quick! I think this is Mom. You gotta go, quick!" said Frank urgently.

"But why?" Andy asked, "I would love to meet your mom."

"She will ask many questions like, where do you live? Where do you study? What do your parents do? We need to prepare you for these kinds of questions." Frank heard the engine of the pickup stopped. "But we don't have time for that right now, you really need to go!"

Both quickly took off their coats and shoes. Andy ran upstairs holding his wet shoes in his hands.

Frank said, "I need to hide these. You know the way out! I will see you soon, my friend."

"Thank you, Frank!" said Andy, smiling, "I haven't had this much fun in a long time!" Then he turned his back and continued running upstairs.

7

A GREAT PLAN

"Who is Mike?" Frank asked to Andy while they were watching *Star Wars: Episode II – Attack of the Clones* in Aurora Shell on Frank's laptop. This had become their routine now. For the past two months, Andy would come over and they would spend time in Aurora Shell. They would read together, talk, watch a movie or surf the Internet. Frank would lock the door to make sure his parents wouldn't walk in and see Andy.

Andy dropped the popcorn he was about to put in his mouth when he heard Frank's question.

"How do you know about Mike?"

"I just saw his name on that cradle in your house," Frank shrugged.

"Oh, I see," said Andy and stopped the movie by hitting the space button. "He was my older brother. I never met him. He died two months after he was born."

"Oh, I'm sorry!" Frank said immediately. "I didn't want to upset you."

"No, it is OK. As I said, I never knew him. But they said that before he died my mom was a very happy person. Apparently, she was caring and cheerful. But after Mike died, she started drinking and smoking a lot. For me, she has mostly been mean, angry, and always sick."

They sat on the cushions, next to each other, quietly.

"Sometimes I get really mad at her," Andy broke the silence. "Like when she yells at me or pushes me across the room. Also, she sometimes forgets to cook. Then, I make cereal or I microwave some square puffs with butter. I know how to make omelet too! Did you know when you add a little bit of milk in egg, the omelet turns out to be fluffy and delicious?"

Frank was in shock of what he just had heard. "Has your mom ever hurt you? My mom would never do that."

Andy shrugged. "Well, I understand her, you know. She can't help it. She lost my brother and she doesn't like me as much as she loved him. I've accepted the truth." Andy looked down and bit his lower lip.

"What about your father, Andy? Maybe he can help her?" Frank was desperately trying to find a way to make his friend feel better.

"Hah…" Andy laughed. "After Mike died, I think they also started to fight a lot. I was not enough to bring them together. Apparently, my father left home when I was just two months old. Each time my mom gets drunk, which is pretty much every night, she blames me for that."

"Blames you for what?" Frank asked, right before he started to chew a handful of popcorn.

"For my father leaving," said Andy, as if the answer was obvious.

"But…Do you think it was really your fault?" Frank asked.

"No, of course not. I was just a baby. But…This is what my mom believes, and her complaining keeps her alive, so…I go with it.".

Andy pushed the space button back again, put a handful of popcorn in his mouth. and they continued watching the movie. Frank was really impressed by how mature and positive Andy was. *I wish I could be like him*, he thought, no wonder he has so many friends, he is very likeable and strong. Andy would constantly talk about his friends at school and in his Thrones – a game similar to chess in Frank's universe – team. Now Frank could make sense of how Andy was capable of making friends so easily.

Maybe, Frank thought, *maybe, I could learn something from him.*

"Oh wow, look at that boy. He is going to be trouble!" said Andy.

"Which boy?"

"That one with the braided hair." Andy was pointing at the screen.

"Oh, Anakin Skywalker. How do you know?"

"I can hear it in his words. He talks back a lot, he doesn't respect his master. That is never a good sign. There is this kid in my school, Leroy, he always talks back to Mrs. Adkins, always makes fun of her. He is also a bully to everyone. I really hate that kid," Andy said in disgust.

"You are actually good at this! He does turn to dark side, the evil side," Frank said excitedly.

"See. I'm good at guessing human behavior."

"Do you think so? So, how about me?"

"What do you mean?" Andy raised his eyebrows.

"I mean what do you think about my character?" said Frank.

"Oh, that. Well, you are definitely not turning to the dark side anytime soon," Andy laughed.

"I'm serious," insisted Frank.

"OK. So…You are obviously smart and you like learning. Knowledge would be your superpower if you were a superhero!"

"Hahaha nice!" said Frank proudly.

The movie was still going and they had almost finished their first bucket of popcorn when suddenly Andy continued, "But also, you are sad. Sometimes you stare into space and your eyes lose their…Hmm…How can I say? They lose their joy for a second or so. Then, you come back to the real world."

Frank thought for a second if that was true. "Well, there is something I have recently learned. It made me really upset. Maybe that's why."

"What is it?" Andy stopped the movie again and moved the empty bucket from his lap onto the floor. He seemed like he was really concerned.

"I heard my parents talking downstairs about me." Frank's eyes had lost their joy again. He was now staring at his laptop, not looking directly at Andy. His lower lip quivered as if he was ready to burst into tears any moment.

"And?" Andy asked impatiently.

"And…Apparently, I'm not their real child," Frank said sadly.

"What do you mean real? You look real to me!" Andy smiled.

"I mean I'm not their child. I was adopted! Don't you understand? My real parents didn't want me." Frank choked down his tears.

"Oh…" Andy thought a couple of seconds before he talked, "So, who are your real parents then?"

Well, that was the same question Frank had kept wondering about since he learned the fact that he was adopted. But he was also afraid to find out something that he was not ready for. His birth parents hadn't wanted Frank for some reason. What was that reason? Why was he unwanted?

Frank shrugged. "I don't know."

"Maybe you can ask your adoptive parents, I'm sure they will have an answer one way or another!" said Andy.

"No way. I can't tell them that I know. They are really not getting along well these days anyway. I don't want to tell them now."

"Hmm…Then that leaves us with only other choice! We have to investigate it ourselves!" said Andy excitedly.

"How? Like detectives?" now Frank was getting excited, too.

"Exactly my friend! Like Sherlock and Watson," said Andy and got up.

"Wait! You have Sherlock and Watson in your universe?" asked Frank in awe.

"Of course, the Sherlock series is my favorite. He is like combination of both of us. He reads emotions and behaviors, then he connects the dots with his smart brain."

"Awesome! So where do we start?"

"Does your mom or dad have an office? Grownups love to keep their important documents in their office."

"They do! It's by the garage," Frank replied.

"Oh, haha! That room used to be an office in our house too; now it is just a storage."

Andy started to think.

"So, what is the plan?" Frank said and got up on his feet, ready to go.

"Well, we need to go in there and check every drawer, every folder. Also, we might have to get in your parents' computer." Andy said this with a concerned voice.

"You say it like it is so easy!" Frank sounded scared.

"Do they have passwords set for their computer?" Andy asked.

"I don't know, really. I've never tried!" Frank was surprised by the question.

"Hmm…When can we go in there?" Andy asked. He looked like he was deep in thought.

"Maybe tonight? After they fall asleep?" Frank started to feel nervous in his stomach.

"Hmm…that would be school time for me. Hmm…" Andy started walking back and forth in Aurora Shell. "I will tell my mom that I'm not feeling well and I can't go to school. It is not my thing – I don't like lying – but we have an important mission! So, I can lie for once."

"Are you sure?" Frank asked worriedly.

"Yes, absolutely! Frank, tonight, we are getting into your parents' office! Be ready. I will be here at midnight your time, but now I gotta go, sorry. So what time is it now?"

"Umm…" Frank checked his watch. "4:42."

"Cool! I will see you in less than eight hours then! Thanks for the movie!" Andy got into the wormhole quickly.

"But…We haven't finished the movie yet…You hadn't even seen the best part!" Frank's disappointment was obvious.

"We will, don't worry. Now, we need to focus on our mission for tonight. I need to make a plan." He crawled deeper into the wormhole and gave Frank one last look, "See you soon Frank."

Five minutes before midnight, Frank was wide awake in his bed, under his blanket. Staring at the clock and counting down the minutes. He was scared and nervous at the same time. What if his parents woke up and heard him in the office? How could he explain that? What if the information that they were looking for weren't there in the first place? This was really risky. Butterflies were flying in Frank's stomach as he thought about it more and more. "This is a bad idea," he said to himself.

Suddenly he heard voices in his closet. Frank slowly got up and sat on his bed. The doors of Aurora Shell opened with a squeak. But it was too dark to see what was inside.

"BOO!" Andy jumped out of the closet to scare Frank.

"Jeez! What the heck are you doing? You scared me!"

"Were you expecting someone else tonight? Are you making friends from other universes and not telling me Frank?" Andy was laughing now, too loudly.

"Shh! You are going to wake them up," Frank whispered.

"I'm sorry!" Andy approached Frank. Now Frank could see Andy's face, thanks to the moonlight filling his entire room. There must have been a full moon that night.

"What happened to your face?" Frank was horrified to see Andy with a black eye.

"Oh, don't worry. Nothing serious...I told mom I wasn't feeling well and didn't feel like going to school today. Then she saw me in the kitchen jumping up and down, playing with Love. She got really mad and called me a liar...Hey, I told you Frank, I'm terrible at lying." He shrugged.

"Does it hurt?" Frank asked, getting closer to him to get a better look.

"Not anymore." Andy smiled and lifted his arm to show Frank what he was holding. "Look what I have!" Andy was shaking something in his hand.

"What is this?" Frank was curious now.

"Our investigation kit!" Andy opened the backpack he was holding and took out two flashlights, some string cheese, a USB, and a tablet.

"That's my tablet!" screamed Frank.

"Well, I told you I don't have one, so I borrowed it from your Aurora Shell just now...For this mission only, don't worry." Andy grinned.

"What are we gonna do with that anyway?" Frank was confused about the plan.

"Let's say we found the documents we are looking for. We can't take them with us, they would notice, right? So..." Andy was looking at Frank with excitement and pride.

"So, we will take their photos! Smart!" said Frank.

They gave each other a high five.

"OK. I get that we have the USB just in case we find something on the computer. But…Andy…Umm…What are the cheese sticks are for?" Frank was holding the string cheese in his hands and shaking them.

Andy was stuffing everything back inside the backpack. "Well, we don't know how long we will spend in the office, do we? What if we get hungry?" Andy grabbed the string cheese from Frank's hands and put it back into the backpack. "This was the only type of food I could think of that wouldn't leave crumbs behind. I thought about apples, too but they make a lot of noise."

"It is almost scary how in detail you thought this thing through," said Frank nodding his head.

Andy shrugged his backpack on and started walking towards the closed bedroom door. Then he stopped and turned back to Frank, smiling with excitement. "Are we going or what?"

Frank turned the door knob quietly and checked the hall way. Everything was quiet. "Follow me!" Frank whispered to Andy.

They started walking down the stairs, taking one step at a time. Andy was three steps behind Frank, constantly checking his behind and around them.

When they came in front of the office door, they were both really nervous.

"Are you ready?" Andy whispered.

"No, not at all," answered Frank with a shaky voice.

"Do you want to find out who your real parents are?"

Frank sighed. "I do."

Andy went ahead and opened the door slowly. It was a white sliding door with glass windows. Someone could definitely see what was happening inside. Andy opened his backpack and took out a flashlight and gave it to Frank. Then, he took the other one himself.

Frank whispered, "So, where do we start?"

"You take the desk and I will check the file cabinet in the corner. Don't forget to be quiet!"

They both tiptoed to the opposite sides of the room. The floor was squeaky but it wasn't as bad as it was in Andy's home, Frank thought. The top drawer of the desk had stationary – some sticky notes, a pair of scissors, tape, and paper clips. It didn't look like a drawer that would contain any kind of important documents. The second drawer had some papers but they were all bills and contract-looking things. There was a speeding ticket with his father's name on it, which Frank knew nothing about. Then he found an old check with *personal loan* written on it. It looked like a lot of money.

"Found anything yet?" Andy whispered from across the room.

"Nope. You?" Frank asked.

"Nah," Andy was determined, though, "We will find it Frank, just keep looking."

The last drawer at the bottom of the desk was locked. Where could the key be? Frank checked out the top of the desk. It was very organized and tidy. He reached for the box that had business cards in it. It was half empty, no keys. Then he checked the pen cup. It was full of pens and pencils. He emptied the cup and it made a loud sound.

Andy shined his flashlight at Frank, "What are you doing? You will wake them up!" he whispered.

"Sorry, I didn't think pens would make so much noise," Frank whispered back. "Also, can you stop shining that light in my face, do you want to make me blind?" He was trying to cover his eyes with his hands.

When Frank looked down at where the pens had spilled, he saw a small golden key shining under the moonlight. He grabbed the key with excitement and put it in the drawer's keyhole. It was the right key! He turned it slowly counter clockwise, and something *clicked*.

The drawer popped out.

There were so many things inside. Lots of documents and photo albums. He didn't know where to start. "Andy!" Frank called his name excitedly, "I think I might have found something! Come up here and help me." Soon both of them were sitting on the ground, looking at the documents they had found.

"I've found your vaccination report. I don't even know where mine is…" Andy said.

"And I found my father's college diploma. I didn't know he had two majors!" Frank was surprised and felt proud for a tiny fraction of a second.

"Your parents' marriage certificate. They got married in Lawrence, Kansas. How romantic!" Andy was smiling.

"That's where they went to school, I guess. His diploma says *The University of Kansas*." Frank was reading everything he found.

"Frank! Look at this!" Andy got excited.

Now they were both reading the same document named *CERTIFICATE OF ADOPTION*.

"This must be it!" Frank whispered.

They continued reading through the document silently. Suddenly Andy broke the silence. "There are no names here. It is just the names of your adoptive parents. Keep looking, Frank. Take this half of the pile and I will take the rest."

Andy handed out a big pile of paper to Frank. They lay on the floor and started reading the papers with the help of their flashlight.

After a few minutes Andy said, "Hey, I don't know you but I'm ready for a string cheese!" Andy's eyebrows were moving up and down, in a funny way.

"You look so strange when you do that," said Frank.

"Like that?" Andy was now moving his eyebrows even faster while he was taking a big bite from the cheese.

They were both laughing when they heard a sound outside. They both turned off their flashlights right away. That same moment, Frank realized that they had left the office door open. He tried to tell that to Andy with gestures but it was too late. The kitchen light was on now, making Frank and Andy visible. They were both scared and didn't know what to do. All the papers and folders were lying on the floor. There was no way they could clean that mess up without being seen. They both crawled under the desk to hide.

"It's my dad! He must have woken up for water or something," Frank said nervously. His mouth was dry.

Andy was shaking and biting his nails. "I don't know how we could explain who I am and what I am doing here, Frank."

They were both sweating and praying for Frank's dad to go to bed before he got to his office. Then suddenly, lights went off. Frank could hear his father's steps. He always shuffled his slippers when he walked. That's how he knew it was his dad. The footsteps finally went upstairs. Then they heard a door open. They did not move out of their hiding place until they heard the door shut.

"Dude…" said Andy with relief, "I think I swallowed the whole cheese when the light went on. I can feel it in my stomach, it is just sitting there."

"Phew, that was close, Andy. We need to hurry."

They were back to reading. A few anxious minutes later, Frank finally found what he was looking for. "Andy!"

Andy and Frank started reading this pretty new looking short letter in dead silence:

STATE OF KANSAS
Kansas Commission for Human Services
Department of Human Services
Kennedy Memorial Office Building
Mailing address: PO Box 54682
Lawrence, Kansas

Hillary J. Robinson
Director of Human Services

Joseph R. Middleton
26 Park Ave.
Indianapolis, Indiana

Dear Mr. Middleton,

We are writing in response to the letter in which you state that you are an adoptive parent and that you are interested in finding your adoptee child Frank's – born as Edward D. Junior – biological mother and father.

Our agency will only allow the adoptee and the biological parents to register if they both wish to find each other. According to our records, Frank's family showed interest in getting in touch. Therefore, we are glad to inform you that we can disclose their contact information to you. However, we do not encourage misbehavior such as harassment or any trips without an appointment.

Here is the contact information of the birth family:
Mother: Mary D. O'Malley
Address: 451 Fremont St. South Dakota 57001
Phone: 605 774 1336
Father: Robert Davis Wilson
Address: Idaho Maximum Security Institution, 13400 Pleasant Valley Rd, Kuna, ID 83634
Phone: 208 338 1635

Please read and sign our confidentiality agreement attached and turn it in to our center no later than 30 days after its issue date.

Regards,
Hillary J. Robinson

"Your name was Edward? It sounds like an old person's name," Andy smiled.

Frank hadn't cared about his old name so much. He was worried about something else. "Idaho Maximum Security Institution," Frank muttered, "My dad…is in prison?"

"Maybe he was there by a mistake? A lot of innocent people go to prison every day, I watch documentaries about it."

This time Andy's efforts to make Frank feel better weren't working. "He could be a thief or murderer. My birth father is a criminal…Great!" Frank rolled his eyes in frustration.

"How about your mother?" Andy asked curiously. "Are you going to call her? You should call her."

"I don't know..." Frank frowned and paused. "I was so excited about finding my real parents but now, I don't even feel... happier. Not even a little bit. I really don't know what to do."

Suddenly something caught Frank's eye. "Look at the date! This letter was sent just this year. Why would dad want to learn about my birth parents all of a sudden?" Frank looked at Andy.

Andy shrugged. "No idea, friend."

"Were they planning to give me back?" Frank's eyes were teared up, looking at Andy.

"Hey, you are not a piece of furniture that people give away once they are bored of it. So, stop those crazy thoughts right now. We got what we wanted so we need to get out of here as soon as we can, then we will talk about it later. Let's take a photo of the paper and put everything back where they belong, in the same order. Then, we will go to bed, have a good sleep. I promise we will talk about this first thing tomorrow and figure things out." Andy held Frank by the shoulders, and he shook him firmly. "Deal?"

"Deal," Frank replied in a defeated, sad voice.

After picking everything up and putting the files back where they belonged, they tiptoed back upstairs and closed the door.

Andy gave Frank's tablet back and grabbed him from the shoulder. "Don't feel sad Frank. Look, I have a tough mom. It is really hard living with her. And look at you! You suddenly have four parents, and at least two of them love you and care about you. Cheer up! We will find them and you will get your answers, tomorrow." He put his backpack on. "But for now, kokoronko!"

Frank's sad mood changed instantly with that last word. "Kokoronko?! What does that even mean?"

"Oh, it means 'goodbye' in Bilthuan language," Andy replied. "It is the most common third language in my universe. They teach us in school, I really like it. Anyway, gotta go, see you tomorrow Frank!"

"See you Andy..." Frank sat on his bed sadly and watched his friend entering Aurora Shell, "Hey Andy!"

Andy turned in the dark and looked at Frank over his shoulder.

"Thank you...I'm really lucky to have a friend like you," said Frank and smiled.

"No problem, friend. Get some rest. See you soon." Andy soon disappeared into the closet.

"Kokoro!" Frank yelled behind him.

Andy laughed in the dark and his voice echoed in the wormhole. "It is kokoronko, not kokoro! Hahaha."

"Whatever," Frank muttered, getting into bed.

That night, Frank couldn't sleep. He kept thinking about what his birth parents would look like and sound like. How he could have lived a different life. Why didn't they want him in the first place? Or, most importantly, why didn't they love him? He needed some answers and he needed them now.

So, he made a plan.

8

JOURNEY

"Are you out of your mind?" Andy just couldn't believe what he had just heard.

"Trust me, I know what I'm doing," said Frank, determined. He was packing up his clothes and his tablet as he was talking to Andy.

"So, genius, tell me! Do you know anything about my world? Why don't you try to find your birth parents in your own universe? You have their address, phone numbers and all. You don't even know if they exist in mine!"

"They must exist. Look…Remember, I didn't disappear in your universe like your cat did in mine. That probably means Love never existed in this universe in the first place. But my biological mother and father are the ones who gave me their DNA, and I did not disappear. So, they must exist. I mean, they might be dead. But I guess I will figure it out! I will find them dead or alive." He shouldered his backpack.

"This is just a theory, though. Maybe we should do some research first?"

"Andy, I don't have time. I want to find out the truth. I can't think about anything else. It is affecting my school. Can't even read anymore. The only thing I think about is my actual parents."

"I just don't understand why you don't want to find them here, which makes a hundred percent more sense!" Now Andy was calmer but still his hands were on his hips, looking down at Frank.

Frank's face had changed from determined to sad as he sat on his bed. His backpack strap slipped off his left shoulder, gently landing the bag on his comforter. He put his hands between his knees like an embarrassed child who just broke an expensive vase. Without even looking at Andy he said, "Because… They didn't want me in this universe. Maybe they will want me in yours?"

Andy could feel his friend's sadness. He sat right next to Frank and put his arm around him, "Look, I understand, I really do. I just want you to be prepared…" At that moment, Andy had a great idea. "Hmm… You know what, this plan could work. But, only on one condition."

Frank inclined his head and looked at Andy with curiosity. "Which is?"

"I'm coming with you!" Andy smiled.

"But…Your mother will notice that you are gone and she will be worried. She might call the police."

"Nah," Andy said, "She wouldn't care. She might not even notice that I'm gone, honestly. But I will leave a note saying that I'm safe and will be back! You should think about yours by the way. What are your parents going to say?"

"I have a theory, and if it is true, I will be fine. If not, which is a slight chance, I will be in so much trouble."

"And your theory is…?"

"Remember, whenever I visit you, the time stops in my universe, it also happens to you when you visit mine. Which I couldn't figure out why or how by the way." Frank grabbed the glass on his bed stand that was half full of water and drank it all. "But, when you are in yours and I'm in mine, I mean, when we are in the universes that we belong to, then the time flows as it should." He delicately set the empty glass on the nightstand.

"Interesting! Never thought of that. Good that we got that covered then. My point is…My universe, my rules! I would be the perfect guide for you, think about it! You don't know the places, transportation system. Even our money looks different than yours. Each bill is in a different color." Andy grew happier, as he thought about his plan more. It just made perfect sense! Not only because he was going to help his best friend, but also, he was going to be away from his mother for a while. No chores and errands.

"I guess you are right. I could use your help!" Frank smiled, "So, what now?"

"If you are ready, let's go to my room. I need to pack and we can look up your parents on the Internet and see what we get!"

"Sounds like a plan," Frank replied, "Umm…But I have to do one more thing before we leave."

"What now? Are you going to go get a cinnamon cookie?"

"No, don't be silly. I want to say goodbye to my mom and dad. Stay here!"

"Oh, bummer. I could use a cinnamon cookie," Andy said.

Frank opened his door and right before leaving the room, he turned to Andy and whispered, "I will be right back!"

He slowly walked into his parents' bedroom. They were both asleep. He just realized that he hadn't been in this room very often. Maybe a couple of times, not more. He noticed a lot of photos on the wall. One of them was taken during a trip to Niagara Falls two years ago. He remembered his mom being worried because Frank had gotten really wet. Frank also remembered how he had learned about potential energy that the water had due to its height and then as the water fell, how it turned into kinetic energy.

"So, energy is always there, Frank. It has always been and it always will be," his father had said to him.

Frank thought maybe his father, Joe, was the reason why he was so into science. His father would take him to the science fairs, museums, buy him science journals and would always tell him not to believe in anything blindly. He always told him to question things.

Frank suddenly felt sadness filling in his heart. He was about leave them. Yes, they had been fighting a lot lately and he was angry that they lied to him. But…They had always been caring, loving and fun and Frank felt thankful for that. "I'm sorry…" he whispered in the dark to his parents. He thought to himself, *I just need to find my birth parents. You even thought about giving me back, I heard you downstairs. Maybe you don't even want me anymore.*

Tiny drops of tears were streaming down his face when he left their room. He wiped his tears as he didn't want his best friend to see him like this. When he got back into his room, Frank found Andy sitting patiently in Aurora Shell.

"Ready?" asked Andy.

"Ready," replied Frank.

With short but quick steps, they both crawled into Andy's room. They stood in the middle of the red carpet and dusted off their clothes. Frank said, "So, I guess we need to find their address first."

"Yep. There is this website where if you pay a small amount of money, they tell you people's addresses and phone numbers." Andy grabbed a chair and sat in front of his computer and started typing.

"But…Where are we going to get that money?" asked Frank.

"I have some." Andy took out a credit card from his backpack, placed it on his desk and continued typing on the computer.

Frank looked at the shiny blue surface of the card from a distance. *Was that Love's picture on it?*

"Wow! You have a credit card? How come your mother let you have one?"

"Oh, this is a common thing here. Every kid has one. Because once you are over ten years old, you have to work in the afternoons at least for a couple of hours. The money we earn goes directly into our account. So, I saved some! Don't worry, we can both use it." Andy winked at Frank and then continued typing.

"So, after school, if you are working, how do you find time to play sports? Or do your other stuff?"

"Hmm…Our schools are different from each other, I guess. In every school, there is a mandatory two-hour socializing time." Andy continued talking to Frank while he was focused on the computer screen. "Every day we take our turn as a team leader to come up with a different activity. We teach it to the group and then we do it together. I created my own ball game once. It was fun!"

Frank couldn't believe what he just heard. Although he highly doubted that he would be good at it, the idea of this school activity system just sounded great.

"And that's it!" Andy shouted.

Frank ran up next to his friend. "Where? Did you find their addresses?"

"Uh-huh. And there's good news, my friend, your father doesn't live in a prison here!"

"Yes!" Frank jumped. "I knew it! C'mon let's go!" he ran straight to the door.

"OK. Frank, please calm down. I know you want to meet them as soon as possible. But it is going to be a long trip. They live in the other side of the city. We need supplies."

"What kind of supplies? Do we have a map?"

"Yes, of course! We have my watch and your tablet" Andy winked at Frank.

"When you wink, it looks creepy. Did anyone tell you that?"

"Ah, I must have a piece of dust in my eye,"

"What dust? From the wormhole?"

"Stardust! Hahaha!" Andy clearly thought this was a pretty good joke.

"Just to let you know, that was a terrible joke," Frank said but couldn't help it and laughed as well. He was just so happy and excited about their upcoming journey. "Wait, why are you packing sunscreen? It is winter."

"Oops! I forgot to tell you. Our winters are pretty warm here. Like upper 60s."

"Great!" Frank was upset now. "Well, what am I going to do now? I have my boots and sweater and like this super warm winter coat, which is killing me already!"

"No worries, I will give you something. Or we could go back to your room if you like?"

"No, it's too risky to go back. I guess I will borrow your clothes. What do you have?"

"OK. I have two clean T-shirts. Which one do you want? I have one with an astronaut on it and the other one has puppies."

"Umm…Astronaut one please."

"What is wrong with puppies?"

"I…I don't know?!"

"Just messing with you! Relax. You got it."

Andy gave the red astronaut shirt and Frank put it on quickly. After a moment of silence, Andy couldn't help but asked, "What are you going to do if they already have you, Frank? How are you going to explain to them where you came from? And what if they don't want a second Frank? Or Edward, I guess…"

"I know, that worries me, too…But I have to try it, Andy. They wouldn't turn away their own child, would they?" Frank's excitement was gone quickly.

"I don't know Frank. They already did that once…" Andy zipped his backpack and put it on.

Once they all packed what they needed, they left the room quietly. They both were extra cautious while going downstairs. Andy left a short note on the kitchen table and grabbed two big plastic bottles of water from the fridge. They could hear that Andy's mom was watching TV when they left the house. Andy locked the door from outside and put the keys in his pocket. "Let's go, my friend!"

It is a lovely day, Frank thought, *birds are chirping, the suns are shining…* Frank was immediately shocked by what he just thought about and what made him say it. "Wait, what?"

"What happened?"

"This is amazing! Just like in *Star Wars!*"

"What are you talking about?"

"You have two suns, Andy!" said Frank with excitement, pointing at their direction.

Andy was not sure if he knew what "the sun" meant.

Frank continued to explain, "Remember my Aurora Shell? There were planets and stars hanging and there was nothing at the center? That was where the sun was supposed to be. The big, hot star that gives the light and heat we need in my universe, in my galaxy, in my solar

system. And you have two of them! How awesome is that!" Frank's mouth was open, he couldn't believe his eyes.

"Oh, that's the magda and the depix. The depix is the smaller one. Now I remember the posters on your wall, that makes sense." Andy looked at his watch. "Hey Frank, if we want to catch the bus, we gotta go now."

"Oh, OK. Sorry!" Frank and Andy started to take faster steps.

Frank couldn't help but keep looking around because he didn't want to miss anything in this different universe. He was constantly glancing around looking at things and taking pictures with his tablet like a tourist. Many things were very similar to his universe, such as houses, people, cars. Cars looked slightly different, though, and they had brands that Frank had never seen before.

"Huh." Frank said with a crooked smile.

"What's up?"

"I always thought I would see flying cars in your universe for some reason."

"Oh yeah, I did, too. I mean, in your universe. I guess they are in all fiction books and movies," Andy looked and smiled.

"Are these all electric cars?" He pointed at the cars parked in the street.

"Yep! Great for the environment, they say. We never had enough oil in the world to begin with." Suddenly, Andy pointed at somewhere two blocks ahead, "This is our bus Frank! Run!"

They ran as if a T-Rex was chasing them for lunch and luckily, they just made it to the bus stop when the bus was just about to close its doors. They sat in one of the back seats. There were only a few people on the bus and they were all looking at them in a strange way.

"Phew, that was close," said Andy.

"Why are people looking at us like that?" asked Frank.

"Hmm maybe because we are a couple of 11-year-olds with backpacks who are taking an interstate bus without grown-ups?"

"Wait, interstate? I thought we were travelling in the same city?!"

"Relax. Yes. But it is close to the northern state border. This was the fastest way."

"Did you just scan your watch on the bus as a ticket? I didn't see you use a card or anything."

"Nope, the machine just scanned my eyes."

"Whoa! I thought that was only in movies!"

"It's cool, isn't it? They catch a lot of criminals this way. You just have to register your retina once at this machine that looks like an ATM, then it recognizes you and connects to your account automatically."

"Nice! And what does that do?"

"This?" Andy was holding a small red rubber ball. "Hmm... With this, you can read people's minds!"

"Whoa!!" Frank was blown away again.

Andy was laughing out loud, "I'm joking, Frank. This is just a ball. I like to play with it when I'm bored, that's all."

"Not funny!" Frank crossed his arms and looked the other way. He didn't like to be fooled by his best friend.

"Come on!" Andy poked Frank's arm. "So, genius. Tell me…" Andy was throwing the ball up and catching it again. "When I throw the ball up, why doesn't the ball fall backwards? We are moving on a bus and it is pretty fast, but it lands straight in my hands each time. Why?"

Frank cleared his throat and looked at Andy. "It is the velocity."

"Meaning?"

"Speed…So…The bus has a horizontal speed this way," he was pointing at the direction of the bus. "You have the same horizontal speed as the bus, and so does the ball you are throwing upwards. So, there is no reason for the ball to change its horizontal location because both the bus and you and the ball are traveling the same distance in equal time at the same speed." Frank pushed back his glasses that were falling off of his nose proudly and smiled at Andy.

"Wow!"

"Did you get it?" Frank was smiling so big.

"Nope. But it cheered you up, and that was my whole purpose."

Frank smiled, "Thanks. You know what makes me happy I guess."

Frank was watching outside when he saw people kissing each other, almost all the time. Like, a lot of them.

"Andy, I see people kissing each other on the cheeks a lot here. What's up with that?"

"Oh, it is a way of greeting people here. I've read in this book once that it is common in hot climates for people to hug and kiss each other more."

"Interesting."

"What about in your dimension?"

"Oh, we definitely need some space. This is a little too much. I'm so glad that you didn't try to kiss me when we first met, I might have punched you in the face."

They both laughed.

Almost an hour had passed when Andy grabbed Frank's arm and woke him up from where he had fallen asleep against the window, "This is our stop, Frank."

When they got off the bus, Frank figured they were not in a suburban area anymore. They were right at the heart of the city.

"Oh no!" Andy said. He was looking inside his backpack and searching for something.

"OK. Now, what did we forget?"

"Food…And I'm starving!" Andy sounded really frustrated.

"Well, if we have enough money, we could eat at that diner right there!" Frank pointed at a diner across the street.

"Sure, we could do that," said Andy. He was so hungry that he could eat anything.

The diner looked more like a candy store with its pink walls and white window frames. The neon sign read *Tyler's Diner* but the letter 'T' was flickering which Frank found almost hypnotizing.

When Andy and Frank entered the diner, a bell rang and for a second, everybody looked at them.

"Awkward," whispered Frank.

They sat at the nearest table. Frank started to read the short menu listed on the board. "Oh, Thank God! You have burgers and fries here too!"

"Can't think of any universe without them," Andy replied.

Frank's eyes caught one of the servers at the next table. She was talking with a young man a little too friendly. "They must be really close," he murmured. Andy turned to see what Frank was talking about and saw this guy giving the server a kiss on the cheek. Remembering their conversation back on the bus, he immediately decided to play a trick on his friend. "Oh, that? This is how they say nice to meet you, here in this part of the city," said Andy.

"Wow. That's a little too much, don't you think?" Frank's eyes were wide open.

"Nah. The opposite. If we don't do it, then they will suspect that we are not from this town!" He leaned towards Frank more and whispered. "We need to act like natives here."

"Hello gentlemen. My name is Mary." Their server was looking at both with a big smile revealing her perfectly white teeth.

"Hello Mary!" said Frank and with a quick move, just stamped a kiss on her cheek. The next thing he remembered was a painful slap on his face.

"Ouch!" Frank yelled in pain.

Andy fell on the floor laughing out loud.

"What is wrong with you, kid?" Mary asked.

"I should ask you the same thing! Ouch!" Frank was holding his red cheek with one hand when he picked up his glasses from the floor. Thank God they were not broken. Without them he was as blind as a bat.

"I'm sorry! Hahaha! I'm sorry, Mary!" Andy finally managed to stop laughing and speak. "My friend is new in this country and he saw everyone kissing to greet each other. He was trying to be kind to you. We apologize, really."

Mary, still confused and a little upset, apologized, "Sorry for hitting you, does it hurt?"

"No." Frank said, still holding his red cheek. "I'm sorry...I was just–"

"Let's forget that. Misunderstandings happen all the time. Now, do you know what you want to order or do you need a couple more minutes?"

"Can I get a burger with fries? With ketchup please?" Frank asked.

"Sure. Ketchup is on the table right by the window by the way. What about you, sir?"

"I would like a chicken sandwich, please," said Andy, "Oh, can we add bacon to mine?"

"Sure thing. That'll be right up." Mary walked toward the kitchen.

"My mom never lets me eat bacon, I guess she doesn't like the smell. Now, I can eat as much as I want, yes!" Andy was excited.

"Andy, do you think that was funny??" Frank was boiling with anger.

"I was just joking! I was about to tell you that I was joking but you just jumped on her! Hahaha."

"I can't believe you… You…." Frank couldn't finish his sentence. Mary was coming back to their table with a big glass of orange juice. "Here is a free orange juice for you, as an apology." She smiled and put the orange juice down on the table. "Let me know if you guys need anything else."

Andy waited until she went back into the kitchen to reveal the news to Frank. "I think she likes you!"

"Who?" Frank sounded surprised.

"Mary!" Andy smiled.

"What? No…" Frank looked at Andy as if he said the most unbelievable thing on earth. "Are you serious? Why would you say that?"

"The way she smiles at you and speaks with you. Plus, the free orange juice?" Andy winked at Frank.

"She was just sorry. And she looks like she's in tenth grade or something."

"So, what? Trust me, I'm good at reading people," Andy winked again.

"Yeah, you told me that before…And could you please stop winking? I told you it's creepy."

"Let's do an experiment. I will go the bathroom, and we will see if she stops by at our table. If she is into you, she would find an excuse to talk to you."

"Oh, come on Andy let's eat and go, you don't need to..." But Andy had already left the table for bathroom.

Sigh.

Frank was nervous now. Being without Andy in Andy's universe, even for a second, made him feel extremely uncomfortable for some reason. Then he started thinking about his birth parents. He still didn't know what they looked like. Did Frank look like his dad or mom? What were they going to do when they met him? What was he going to do about his twin in this dimension? He needed a plan. "Think! Think Frank!" he talked to himself while he was watching people outside passing by the window.

"How is your orange juice?" Mary made Frank jump as she had caught him off guard. There she was, right next to Frank with their food.

"Oh! Umm...Great! I guess. I don't think it is fresh, but it tastes good...Sorry...I'm terrible at lying...Umm, thanks again..."

He felt more and more uncomfortable as he spoke. *Maybe I should just shut up!* he thought.

"So, where are you from?" Mary asked.

Uh-oh, here we go, Frank thought. What was he going to say now? He went with the safest option. "Uhm...From not very far..."

"Oh, really? Where exactly?"

"I..." Frank was sweating.

Andy, who had just returned from the bathroom must have heard the question. He answered, "Kanata!"

"Huh. Never been there," said Mary.

Phew. Frank thought. He quickly said, "After high school, I want to move somewhere else for college, though."

Mary kindly put their food on the table. "Why? Don't you like it there?" she said.

"I... I like it. But it is time to explore new places. It gets boring to be in the same city after many years."

"I can agree with that," Mary smiled at Frank. "What are you guys up to?" as she was writing their check.

"Nothing. We're just...Uh...We are on our way to find my parents," said Frank.

Andy cleared his throat. "Ahem...He meant we are on our way to meet his parents. They are visiting. We told them that we were going to have a quick lunch while they were shopping next door."

"Oh, I see." Mary turned at Frank. "Well, enjoy your trip. Here is your check."

She was holding a square shaped paper with some QR Code looking shapes on it, which Andy scanned with his watch and clicked on some buttons. It also had a handwritten note on its back saying, "Thanks! Come again!"

"Please don't forget to give me a star if you were satisfied with your service. Have a great day!" she said and left to help another party who had just arrived.

"How do we give her a star? On social media or what?" Frank was confused.

"Oh no, this is an app that everyone uses these days. Some customer service companies made it mandatory for their employees and customers actually. So, look…" He showed his watch to Frank, while Frank was filling his mouth with French fries. "You can give stars to people if you like them, if they are good or kind to you." Andy looked at his watch closer. "Oh, zazingo! I need to charge my watch." He plugged it into the outlet on the table. *'Oh, zazingo!' must be something like 'Oh, crap!'* Frank thought. He liked that word.

"How about if they are rude to you?" asked Frank with his mouth full, spitting out some fries.

"Gross, Frank cover your mouth!"

"Sorry," he grinned and shrugged.

"No, you can't give bad reviews. If you don't like something, you just don't give any stars. You can only give ten stars a month, and you are not allowed to vote for the same person for three more months. Also, there is a kind of police that is watching who you are giving stars to. If they see a pattern, they investigate for fraud."

"That's brilliant! That way everyone would be nice to each other." He took a sip of his orange juice. "But wait, what do those people get in return?"

"That is the point. Once a person collects a hundred stars, they can turn it into cash. That many stars are equal to something like your ten dollars. Seems like it is working." Andy took a bite from his sandwich and looked at Frank. "So…She likes you, huh?" Andy winked.

Frank blushed. "I guess so…"

"By the way, what were you thinking telling her about our plan, genius?"

"Sorry, Andy. I'm not like you. I don't know how to respond sometimes. How do you manage to be normal when you socialize with people?"

"Hahaha, I guess I'm just being myself. No worries, I got you friend." Andy took another bite and asked, "Do you think a human in one universe can be another thing in another universe?"

"Like a banana?" Frank smiled in his nerdy way. "We share 60% of our DNA with bananas, did you know that?"

"Seriously? Who would have thought!" he swallowed his last piece. "How about monkeys?" he took another big bite.

"I read that we share 96% of our DNA with chimpanzees, which makes sense evolutionarily…"

"Wow, that's a lot! So, you could be a banana in this universe, huh?" Andy laughed.

"Or a chicken. We share 60% of our DNA with chickens as well…Maybe you just ate me, and you don't know."

Andy gulped. "Well, I certainly hope not. That's gross!"

They looked at each other and laughed.

After he finished his food, Andy unplugged his watch and checked the time. "If you are finished, let's get going. We need to walk for a while."

"One sec!" Frank chugged down his orange juice and said, "OK. let's go."

As they were leaving the diner, Andy poked Frank's arm and gestured at something with his head, as if he wanted to draw Frank's attention to that way. When Frank looked, he saw Mary waving at him behind the counter, with a huge smile on her face. Frank hesitantly waved back.

Andy laughed. "Dude, I need to teach you not to blush. It's embarrassing!"

"Stop it already!" Frank was even blushing more now. He shoved Andy out of the diner door.

Their walk in the city was really nice. Different kinds of shops, restaurants, schools, libraries, church looking buildings. They all looked similar to Frank's universe. Until he saw a weird animal crossing the street.

"What is that Andy?" Frank was pointing at a man walking his pet in the park.

"Oh, it is a tet."

"Looks like something between a pig and a dog."

"Hahaha maybe. Never thought of that. You guys don't have them? Well, pigs went extinct a hundred years ago or so. Apparently, there was a sudden epidemic, affected a lot of farm animals but it was brutal for pigs."

"But you ate bacon back in the diner. Wasn't that from a pig?"

"Oh, it was lab grown. I don't know exac–" Andy couldn't finish his sentence since he had just bumped into a man.

"Watch your way kid!" he yelled, "Look what you did for God's sake!" The briefcase he was carrying had fallen and whatever was inside had spilled all around. He was a tall, skinny man with a nice suit on. His hair was greasy and combed back as if he had just dipped his head into a bucket of hair gel. Andy could smell his strong, cheap cologne which reminded him of his art teacher, Mr. Korchevskov. Each time he came by his desk to help with his art work, Andy could smell a mixture of cigarettes, sweat and cologne. They would come in waves, in this exact order.

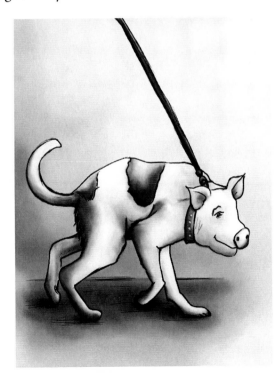

"I'm so sorry sir, I really didn't see you, at all..." As Andy kneeled down to help, he saw a lot of cash and bagged white and green stuff in the briefcase. When he raised his head, he noticed a bump under the man's jacket about the size and shape of a gun.

The man quickly grabbed everything and checked his surroundings to see if anyone was watching. He looked down to Andy and Frank, almost grinning. Something about him was really bothering Andy.

"So, what are you boys doing here alone?" the stranger man asked, "Where are your parents?" He wiped the dust off of his briefcase. "Are you hungry? I could buy you some food. There is a place nearby that makes great pizza!" He said with an evil smile.

Frank responded with all his pure honesty, as always. "We just ate actually thanks! We are looking for my–"

Andy jumped in the conversation. "Our parents are in the car right there."

They all looked where Andy pointed at. There was a couple waiting in a small red car which looked like a Volkswagen Beetle but it was much bigger. The right door opened by folding upwards while Frank watched in astonishment. Andy waved at the people in the car smiling, and the woman in the car waved back, looking surprised. Frank was totally confused about Andy's motives.

"We were just grabbing ice cream for my little brother. Thanks. And sorry again sir, have a nice day!" Andy pulled Frank by the arm. "Frank please keep walking and don't look back."

"Why? What's happening?"

"Didn't you get it? He is a dangerous man. He had a gun and lots of money-"

"He had a gun?!" yelled Frank.

"Then he changed from angry to nice too quickly. Never a good sign!"

"How do you know these things? I didn't see what you saw at all!"

"I don't know," Andy shrugged. "Reading a lot of detective books and reading my mom's moods every day helped, I guess. Come on, we need to make sure he is not following us. Let's go into this mall. Then we can take one of the exits in the back."

The mall had a gigantic white marble entrance. It looked like a palace, almost. The revolving doors were all glass with golden frames. When they entered, Frank saw trees in the mall. Were there also birds? He could hear them chirping. It was almost like an indoors forest. They took the escalators going up. The floor had many stores and restaurants. As they were walking Frank could see that Andy was constantly checking if the strange man was following them or not.

"Is he following us?" Frank asked.

"I don't think so," Andy smiled.

"Hey, what is that store?" Frank asked.

"Oh, that one? We have the same store close to our house. It is an ice cream store with all kinds of flavors and they can 3D print your ice cream in any shape."

"How do they keep the shape? Doesn't it melt?"

"I knew you were going to ask that. No, because they cover it with chocolate right away. It is delicious! Do you want to try?"

"Yes, please!" Frank's eyes were wide open with excitement. His mouth was watering already.

When they walked in the store, there was a short line in front of the counter. It was a colorful store with a purple candy machine in the corner. The floor was black and white checkered. Each table and chair set were of different color. For some reason, Frank remembered Charlie's Chocolate Factory. He had imagined somewhere like this while reading the book. There were framed pictures of were cartoon characters on the wall. Each one of them was holding a different shape of ice cream. Frank had never seen those characters before. One looked like a skunk. The idea of a skunk as an ice cream made Frank giggle. There were no empty seats. *This place must be popular,* he thought.

"Look!" Andy said, pointing at a kid's ice cream. It was in the shape of Powerman.

"Oh, I think I want that one!" Andy said.

Frank looked around to see another interesting one. He saw one that looked like a cat. The other one looked like a book. *Is that a tractor?? Wow,* he thought. He was really impressed with this place. When he looked at the cashier front, he saw this high school kid, loudly joking with his friends and blocking other people's way. *Ugh… They think they are all grown up but they are just being annoying,* he thought. Then Frank's eyes caught what the kid was holding: a giant space shuttle ice cream. "That's it!" Frank said, "That's what I'm getting!"

"Good choice!" Andy winked.

After they paid, they got their ice cream from the cashier.

"Here you go!" the nice-looking cashier lady said, "Enjoy!"

Frank took a small bite. "Hmm…Delicious!"

"Right?" said Andy.

Both left the ice-cream shop, grinning from ear to ear. They both looked like the happiest kids on earth. As planned, they left the mall from a back exit. The door opened to an almost empty parking lot. The map app on Andy's watch indicated the path right in front of them, so they took that narrow trail surrounded by trees. After a while, they found themselves on a street, with pretty houses and parked cars on both sides. Eight or ten blocks later, Andy's watch told them to stop. Now, they were standing in front of a house with a bright red door. The house looked sad from outside. The plants on the patio were half dead. The swing was dusty and corroded. The wood was too old, definitely in need of some repair.

"We are finally here," said Andy.

The sun was already setting, and they didn't have a plan.

"What are we going to do now? I can't just go ring the bell," said Frank.

"We really didn't plan this far, did we?" Andy had this concerned look on his face. He bit his lower lip as he always did when he thought deep. He looked around. "Let's look around the house and see if any lights are on, if anyone is inside," he said.

"Should we split up?"

"No, we should always be together, it is safer that way." He looked at the east face of the house and saw the light. "This way!"

They climbed the squeaky wooden stairs to the patio and tiptoed around the house. They saw moving shadows ahead where the window was. It was at the end of the long, wide patio, maybe twenty feet away or so. They walked slowly towards the window where the light was coming from. The old wood was making too much noise. Afraid of being caught, they started crawling instead. Finally, they made it to the window and hid under it. The window was wide open, and they could hear people talking. Frank and Andy slowly raised their heads and peeked in. The first thing that caught their attention was the fact that the inside of the house was as sad as the outside. No pictures on the walls. *Strange*, Frank thought, *our house is full of photos and paintings.* The house smelled like cigarettes – like, lots of them. The carpet was old, and its hopelessly faded colors matched the walls' gray tone. There was a bald guy, in his thirties or forties, sitting on a sofa right in front of the TV, holding a beer in one hand and a cigar in the other. He burped loudly and made some other weird bodily noises as Andy and Frank watched.

"Yep, definitely this is your father," said Andy and laughed.

"Too funny!" whispered Frank.

This was it. He was looking at his biological father. He wasn't as Frank had pictured. For some reason, Frank had hoped his actual father would look more heroic – wise, young, strong and gentle. The man sitting on the couch looked angry, bored and unhealthy. A sudden thought crossed Frank's mind. *Joe was wise, strong, and gentle.* Despite his frustration, Frank was determined to give it a chance. He was not going to let himself feel discouraged. He didn't come all the way down here for nothing.

There was a woman standing behind the man preparing food who looked really thin and tired. Her red hair was just like Frank's, only hers was longer and weaker. When she turned towards the window and revealed her face, Andy could see her black eye.

Andy immediately understood what was going on in that house. "Oh no Frank, I'm sorry."

"What? Why did you say that now?"

"Ed!" The father roared.

His voice was so cruel and angry that both Andy and Frank jumped in fear. In a few seconds, they heard someone running downstairs. Frank was anxious to see himself in another world. This was the weirdest experience he has ever had in his 11-year-long life. Was he going to be the same? Would he be a straight A student like himself? How about science? Maybe Edward was better at science than Frank was. Suddenly he got jealous of his Edward version. *Don't be silly! Stop thinking about stupid things!* Frank thought to himself.

"Yes, daddy?" Edward stood right in the middle of the living room. He was distant from his father and was looking scared. He was a smaller version of Frank.

"He is so…So skinny and even shorter than me!" Frank was shocked.

When Frank looked at Andy, he saw that his eyes were glued on the father. "What now?" Frank said.

"Frank…He needs to play the 'yes game' to survive this. Otherwise, I know what is going to happen. I'm very familiar, trust me."

"'Yes game?'"

"Shh…" Andy realized that the mother looked toward the window for a second. They both ducked down behind the window, praying that she hadn't seen them.

"Did you finish your homework, kid?" the father asked.

"Yes, Dad."

"OK. Good!" He took a sip of his beer. "Did you also clean your shithole room?"

"Yes, sir."

"Good boy. You know why I work so hard, child?" He got the hiccups while he was talking. "So that you can go to school, become (*hiccup*) a doctor, become rich and look after (*hiccup*) me and your mother. Do you understand?" His voice was so loud that Frank was sure neighbors could hear them easily.

"Yes, Dad."

Frank and Andy peeked in through the window again. Frank turned to Andy. "He is playing the *Yes Game* very well so far, good for him!"

"Good." The father took a puff on his cigar. Immediately he turned red and started coughing. He couldn't breathe. Skinny Frank was standing still in the middle of the room, not knowing know what to do. His mother quickly brought some water for her husband. The water worked but now he was more agitated than ever. While he was trying to take a deep breath, he noticed something Edward was holding. "What is that in your hand, kid?"

Andy whispered to Frank, "Oh no, Frank, this is not good. He needs to run."

Edward answered, "Nothing. Just a popsicle. Mom said I could have one before dinner."

The mother hopelessly attempted to stop the father from getting angry. "It is OK. Rob, let him go. Please, it is just a snack."

"SHUT UP WOMAN!" He hit her with the back of his hand so hard that she fell on the coffee table behind her.

Frank covered his mouth so as not to scream in terror. Both Andy and Frank were worried for the mother and Edward now, but there was nothing they could do. Edward ran to his mother and cried. "Mom, are you OK?"

"Give me that popsicle, you bastard! If I say you can't have anything before dinner, YOU CAN'T HAVE ANYTHING BEFORE DINNER! DO YOU UNDERSTAND ME?" He was holding Edward by the shoulder and literally screaming at his face.

Face turned down, Edward said, "Yes, sir."

"I couldn't hear?!" yelled Rob.

"YES, SIR!" said Edward.

His father wasn't finished with him. He grabbed him around his belly with single arm, lifted him up and opened the front door. Frank and Andy crawled into a darker part of the patio so that they wouldn't be seen.

"Stay outside tonight. That's how you learn your lesson, boy!" screamed Rob, spitting. He locked Edward outside and continued yelling to the mother. Edward's mom begged him to stop, but he was more powerful than her.

Edward sat on the stairs in front of the door. He took his tiny head between his hands and started sobbing.

Frank told Andy, "We need to help him."

"How? If he sees you, he will ask a lot of questions."

"We have no other choice. We can't leave him here like this, in the dark alone. Come on."

They both slowly approached Edward from behind.

Andy whispered, "Pssst. Hey! Ed! Hey!"

Edward couldn't understand for a second where the voice was coming from. He wiped his tears and looked around. Then when he turned back, he saw two silhouettes in the dark. "Who are you?" Edward talked to the darkness.

"I'm Andy, and this is my friend, Frank." They moved one step forward. Now Edward could see their faces thanks to the moon light.

"What are you doing here?"

"Well, it is a long story but we want to talk to you. Is there a place where we can all talk? Away from your father? He scares me a little." Andy smiled nervously.

"Yeah. He scares me too, believe me." He stood up on the stairs. "There is a place." Edward checked them both out as if trying to understand whether they were dangerous or not. "Follow me!" He said.

They walked about fifty steps or so in silence. When they stopped in front of this giant tree Andy and Frank couldn't believe their eyes. In the middle of tens of branches and thousands of twigs, hidden among the rustling leaves, there it was: Edward's tree house.

Edward said, "This is my hiding place."

Andy whispered in Frank's ear, "He has his own Aurora Shell!"

Edward continued, "When my dad gets angry like that I always come here. He doesn't know about this place but my mom does. She knows that I'm safe here." He turned to Frank and Andy. "Do you want to check it out or not?"

"Yeah, sure," said Andy, "Hey, I'm sorry about your dad."

"Thanks." He grabbed the rope ladder. "Each time I think I'm getting used to it, it still feels hard. It is hard to understand him." Andy had already started climbing up the ladder when Edward got closer to Frank under the moonlight. "You look really familiar...Have we met before?" asked Edward to Frank.

"Umm...I don't think so?" Frank felt uneasy and avoided eye contact.

"What is your name again?"

"Frank" he gulped.

"Come on guys!" Andy yelled from above, "I'm already here!"

Both Frank and Edward started to climb up the tree. *Wow, it is really high up,* Frank thought to himself, *better if I don't look down.*

Once Frank entered the tree house, he realized it was huge! Much bigger than his Aurora Shell. There were super hero posters everywhere and piles of comic books were lying around. There were some board games on his desk that he had never seen before.

"Who is Henry Benjamin Clark?" Frank was looking at the giant life size poster of this guy.

"Oh, that is the most famous soccer player on my team, The Folkers," Edward answered.

"Is soccer popular here?" Frank sounded surprised.

"Like the rest of the world, of course!" He turned to Andy, "What is wrong with him?"

Andy smiled, "He is just…From a distant village. Don't worry."

Frank kept looking around the tree house and seemed disappointed. "So, I don't see anything related to science here."

"Science?" Edward laughed. "Dude, I suck at science. I don't understand chemistry, math or any of that crap. I hate them."

Frank was puzzled. "But…Your parents…Haven't they ever bought you science books, magazines, taken you to museums, or told you to question things all the time?"

Edward couldn't believe what he just heard. "Are you kidding me? Did you see my father out there? Did he seem like a museum guy to you? He raised me exactly the way my grandfather raised him – go to school, don't ask questions, do what he says, go wherever he says and help around the house." Edward looked down and played with his shoe lace. His voice was shaky. "I've never played on a sports team, either. He wanted me to go straight to work after school instead of to the soccer practice."

Frank felt so sorry for Edward. He was so different than what he expected, and this wasn't his fault. He suddenly missed his parents Joe and Francine. He just wanted to go home and hug them, thank them for the way they raised him and treated him. Just now, he was able to understand how difficult it can be to have a great family and he already had it. He felt so stupid ever leaving home for this.

"So, what did you want to talk about?" Edward asked from where he was sitting.

"What?" asked Frank.

"You had said you wanted to talk, earlier. What do you want to talk about?"

Frank had no urge to be a part of Edward's family anymore. He didn't know what to say. But then he thought about something he always wondered. "How about your mom? What kind of a person is she?" He asked.

"Oh, my mom is wonderful. She does everything she can to make me a good person. She cares about me a lot." His love for his mother could easily be seen in his eyes. "Oh, you know what, speaking of science, she loves science. She is a physics teacher!"

Andy elbowed Frank and they looked at each other in surprise. *I guess I took after my mother after all*, Frank thought. Learning about his biological mother made him happy. Now, he could picture her whenever he wanted to.

"So, you just wanted to talk about my mom? That's awkward." said Edward, raising his one eyebrow.

"No. Actually, we have just moved into this neighborhood. We were going to ask you who the cool kids are," said Andy.

Frank was amazed one more time with Andy's lying performance.

"Oh, nice! I could introduce you to some of them tomorrow if you like. Kyle lives two blocks away. He is two years older than me, but he is cool. He is my best friend. There are also some others. Yeah, definitely I can introduce you tomorrow, if I don't get grounded," he rolled his eyes.

"We would love that!" said Andy. "You have some cool comics books in your collection!" Andy smiled. "Does your father buy these?"

Edward got up. "Yes and no," he replied. He opened the small desk drawer in the corner. "The electronic stuff that he doesn't use anymore, I collect it here. I sell it, and with the money, I buy the comic books." He picked up a few earphones, cables, cameras to show, then he put them back in the drawer.

Frank thought to himself, *well, he doesn't like science but definitely his mind is working.*

"So, what school do you go to?" Andy asked.

"Minton High. But my mom is also homeschooling me."

"Isn't high school a little old for homeschooling?" Frank asked, surprised.

Andy nudged him sharply with his elbow and just jumped in. "Ahem, what he meant was it must be hard for your mom to catch up with all this high school curriculum stuff." Andy stared at Frank with his angry big eyes. Immediately Frank knew he must have said something wrong. But this was so tough for him. He just didn't know when to say things and when not to.

"Yeah, I guess. She is always tired. I have a baby brother and, he takes most of my mom's time and energy." Edward corrected his glasses in the saddest way possible.

"A brother?" Frank was getting one shock after another.

"Yes, he is so little. Sometimes when my parents fight, he starts crying, and I try to calm him down."

"What's his name?"

"Greyson."

"So, I have a brother here. Well, that feels so strange," Frank whispered to himself.

"What did you say?" Edward was looking at him.

Andy interrupted again. "He was saying that you are lucky. You will have someone to talk with, or play soccer with."

"Yeah, but I need to wait like years for that, and when he is eleven, I will be twenty or so by then. I'm hoping to not be around my parents when I'm in my twenties."

"Eddie!" Edward's mother was calling from outside.

"My mom is here!" Edward was panicking now. "I have to go guys! She must be worried."

"Edward! Are you there?"

"Yes Mom! Coming down!" Edward turned to Frank and Andy. "Hey, what are you guys gonna do now?"

Frank and Andy looked at each other not knowing what to say. But as always, Andy came up with something really quickly. "Could we hang out here for a bit before we go home?"

"Yeah, sure," Edward responded, "There are blankets in that box. It gets cold in here in the evening. Very nice to meet you Frank and...."

"Andy. Nice to meet you, too," said Andy.

"Take care of yourself, my friend!" said Frank and waved to him.

"I have to turn off the light, sorry, my mom can't know you're here."

"That's fine, we understand," said Andy.

They could hear him climbing down the ladder. Then they heard his mom speaking, "Who were you talking to?"

"No one."

"Are you OK honey? Let me look at you."

Their voices faded into the night. Andy and Frank looked at each other in the dark. They fell silent, each one of them filling in the silence with their own thoughts. There was only the moonlight in the tree house, but it was enough to see the surroundings and each other's faces. They both wanted to say something but they couldn't. They were both speechless after what they had seen and heard. The night had turned out to be so saddening and almost surreal. Frank had just met himself in another universe. Although they shared the same DNA, he thought that they were absolutely different with Edward. *I never thought that my parents who raised me would affect actually who I am,* Frank thought to himself, *I thought it was all biological.*

They each took one blanket from the dusty box. The blankets smelled like they hadn't been washed for months. They lay down on the pillows and cushions that were lying on the floor. When they looked up, they realized that there were big holes in the roof where the branches poked through, and they could see the beautiful stars through the empty spaces.

"So beautiful," said Andy.

"I know..." Frank smiled. "Did you know that some of them are dead already but we can still see their spark?"

"Wait...What? How?"

"So, the light travels at 186,000 miles per second, but also they are really far away. For example, the closest known star to the sun is the Alpha Centauri triple-star system, and in order to get here from there, it would take more than four years for light to travel. But I don't know your galaxy. It must be totally different. I would love to study that when I grow up."

"Wow! So cool! So, what happens when a star dies?"

"They say it becomes a red giant first."

"Like Hulk? The giant guy we watched together in that movie?"

"No. Probably way bigger than that."

"And it is red? Awesome! And then?" Andy placed his both hands between his cheek and the pillow. He gazed at his best friend, wanting to hear more.

"It collapses into itself and becomes a really heavy, dense object like a black hole or neutron star."

"It is so sad," Andy said, "Such a pretty thing has to die. Every good thing has an end."

"It is not so sad, really. Because if the stars hadn't died, we wouldn't exist today!"

"What do you mean?"

Frank could hardly contain his excitement. "I watched this *Cosmos* series. They say that the elements made inside the red giant – like oxygen, carbon and iron – are spread through space when the star dies. This stardust eventually makes other stars and planets and us. These are the elements we are made from."

"Wow! Dude! You are awesome!" Andy fist bumped Frank.

"Haha! Not me, they are. The scientists in my world." Frank rolled on his back and looked at the stars again. He thought about the things that he didn't know about space and life. There were so many things that were still undiscovered.

"So, you have a brother, huh? Congratulations!" said Andy.

"Yeah, I guess. I think it would be really cool to have a brother." Frank paused for a moment. "It would be even better if he were you." He turned to Andy to see his response.

He could see tears building up in Andy's eyes. Not expecting this reaction at all, Frank felt sad seeing his friend like that and wondered if he had said something wrong again.

"Yeah. That would be really cool…" Andy sighed. "Maybe in another universe?"

They both looked at each other and laughed.

"So, from what I understand, you aren't staying with Edward's family, right?" Andy asked.

"Right..."

"Perfect decision, my friend. That man was mad!"

Then they both turned their backs to each other and curled up in their blankets. They needed to rest before they hit the road the next day. Finally, they were going back home.

"Andy?"

"Yes, Frank?"

"How do you do that?"

"Do what?" said Andy.

They turned around. Now they were facing each other again.

"How do you stay so positive, after you have been through so much with your family?" said Frank. "Look at me, I mean other me; he is sad and scared, as he should be. He is not happy at all, and you both have similar lives. But you are, somehow, always happy."

"Well, not always–"

"But almost always," Frank interrupted. "You know what I mean...How do you do that?"

"Hmm...I've never thought about that. I guess I just love life, and I like people." Andy shrugged. "You can't choose your family and you can't choose your past, but you can choose your future and present. I want to be successful one day and make my mom proud, show her that I'm worthy of something. Also, I want to have a family and be the best father ever. I just don't believe that because I was born unlucky, I should stay that way. I need to find my own way to break the curse and enjoy the journey, you know?"

"You speak like a thirty-year-old man sometimes, my friend. I'm starting to think that you are possessed."

"Hahaha! This isn't the first time I've heard that. I guess I'm old inside."

They both giggled.

"You couldn't get all the answers you wanted today. Are you going to be OK with that?" Andy asked.

"Like what?"

"Like why they gave you for adoption," Andy said.

"Although I don't believe in faith, I would like to think that sometimes everything happens for a good reason. I think I don't want to know that answer anymore, because I don't care."

Andy gave Frank the thumbs up and smiled.

"Good night, my nerdy friend," said Andy.

"Good night, my old-inside-friend!" said Frank.

9

DANGEROUS UNIVERSE

Frank woke up with the sounds of leaves rustling in the wind. Now the suns were up, and sunshine was pouring down through the tall trees onto the open space in the tree house, making it look warmer. He noticed things that he didn't see last night. For example, there was a half-inch layer of dust covering almost everything, and there were some cookies and half a burger sitting on the floor right across from where he slept. Ants were crawling all over them. "Gross!" he whispered to himself. He yawned and stretched.

"We have a problem Frank." Andy sounded nervous.

Frank straightened himself up. Still not completely awake, he rubbed his eyes. "What are you doing?" he asked as he saw Andy emptying their backpacks. Everything was on that dusty floor now.

"We must have forgotten our charger in that diner. And the batteries on both my watch and the tablet are dead!"

"So?"

"So?! How are we going to find our way home? We were following GPS on this! I don't have a map or anything!"

"Why are you so worried? The only thing we have to do is to find the bus stop that goes to Bourn Street. We can ask people around there for directions."

Andy rolled his eyes. "Frank, we can't ask for directions, it is dangerous."

"Why?"

"Two lost kids? They could call the cops or worse, they could try to hurt us."

"Pfft…You are always too worried."

"Well, one of us has to be."

"Can we ask Edward for a charger?"

"There is no way I'm going back to that house of terror."

"Fine. Let me think." Frank was deeply absorbed in thought, trying to find a solution. "When you checked on the map, do you remember if this house was north or south of the bus stop?"

"I think it was south."

"Cool, so we need to head north, keep walking in that direction, and eventually we'll find the highway. We can find the bus stop then."

"OK. Genius, but we don't have a compass."

"Well, let's look around in here. Maybe we'll find one."

"You really expect us to find a compass here?"

"No, actually I want you to look for a clock or watch, with the hour and minute hand."

Andy didn't even ask why. He trusted his friend. He had always found smart ways to solve problems.

They started looking around the tree house and found some really random things. Among them were a plastic sword, lots of old magazines covered in spider webs, and a pair of Christmas socks. Frank opened the small drawer in the desk and yelled with joy, "I think I have found one!" This drawer was the one Edward showed them, the one full of electronic stuff. Cables, more cables, plugs, earphones, Christmas lights, a tool set and two watches. They both were still working and in good shape. One of them was gold, and the other one was silver and black.

"Oh, this is what Edward was talking about. Apparently, he is selling his father's old stuff to make money. Kind of his revenge, I guess. So, what do we do with the watch?" Andy said.

"Let me show you a trick that I learned from my dad. He taught me when we went camping last year." Frank grabbed the golden watch, grabbed his backpack and started going down the rope ladder. He looked up and saw Andy looking at him from above, confused. "Are you coming or not?"

"Yes!" Andy said, still having no clue what was going on. He grabbed his backpack and followed Frank.

"We are lucky that the sky is clear," said Frank happily.

"I still don't know what we are doing."

"Here. This is how you can tell where north is. You point the hour hand, the little one, at the sun. Then you imagine a line passing through between the angle of this direction and the 12 mark on the watch."

Andy looked at the watch, then stared at his friend, his mouth open. "OK. Go on…"

"Then the end of the line facing the Sun will be south and the opposite end will be directing us north. We'll go this way!" Frank winked at Andy.

Andy said, "I thought you hated when I winked."

"I think I'm starting to like it." Frank winked again.

The route looked different from what it had looked like the day before. You could see the small towns in the distance now. Beautiful houses were lined up along the road. They all had tall trees in their yards and ivy-looking plants covered their walls. Frank could swear that he saw those plants moving as if they were growing fast forward. Some of the buildings were very big like mansions with two garages and swimming pools. Another one they saw was very modern looking and made almost entirely of glass, which didn't look very safe to Frank. But where were all the people? They felt strange that no one was around. There were no hints of human life except the cars driving by.

Many minutes of silent walk later, they ended up at a fork in the road.

"Now what?" asked Andy, "Left, or right?"

"Well, as long as we head north, it shouldn't matter. Let's go this way."

They took the path on the left. They were now on a narrow path surrounded by trees on both sides. They both remembered this path.

Andy breathed in the fresh air when trees were magically soaring above them. "I love the smell of pine trees. It makes me happy."

"Well, I'm not surprised about that," said Frank, sarcastically.

After a long but pleasant walk, they finally heard the noise of cars passing by.

"We must be close!" Frank sounded relieved. They were going to be fine.

Andy gave Frank a high-five. "You are the best!"

They both laughed. After passing the mall that they had visited a day before, they walked for a while along the highway in the opposite direction of the traffic. The bus stop was right there, just a few yards away. As soon as they sat on the dirty black plastic seats, Frank took out his water bottle, took a big sip and then offered some to Andy. At that moment Frank realized that there was something wrong with his friend.

"What's wrong? We are going home!" he bumped his elbow against Andy's. "Cheer up!"

"That's exactly the problem," Andy sighed.

Frank had never seen Andy sad before. This was new.

"Hey friend, you know I'm not good at these things…" Frank awkwardly put his arm around his friend's shoulders and he patted him.

"It's just amazing when we spend time together. This whole adventure was so awesome. I learned a lot from you and felt like we could have many more adventures together if we were brothers," Andy sighed. "But we are not and I'm going back to my reality which includes my angry mother who is trying to drink herself to death." In frustration, Andy threw away a flower he'd been fiddling with, which he had absently picked from a crack in the sidewalk at their feet. "She is going to be so mad…I don't want to go back, Frank." Frank could see tears welled up in Andy's eyes.

"I know…" Frank said. "What can I do? Tell me! I would like to help."

"There is not much you can do, really. But thank you. It means a lot." Andy attempted a smile. "By the way, do you mind if I keep the golden watch?"

"Umm…Sure, no problem." Frank was taken by a surprise. He even had forgotten about the watch.

"I was thinking that if I sell it and get some cash, I can give it to mom and maybe she would be less angry with me then."

"Such a great idea!" Frank said. But inside, he felt bad for his friend. He wished Andy didn't have to worry about these kinds of things. He wished Andy's mother was nicer.

"Look! Here comes our bus!" said Frank.

The big blue bus slowly approached the stop. As he watched it getting closer, Frank was torn. He was happy to realize that he actually had a wonderful family. That's why he couldn't wait to go back home. But then there was Andy. He didn't want his best friend, his only real friend, to be sad or upset. He deserved much better. *I wish there was something that I could do,* he thought.

The bus ride was really quiet. Many people on the bus, including Andy was asleep and without his tablet, Frank was really bored. So, he decided to think about what he would do when he got home. Giving a big hug to Mom and Dad was at the top of his list. Introducing Andy to his family was second. But they had to really prepare well for that. He thought about finishing the book he had just started: "The Philosophy Book for Middle Grade." Andy had suggested a book like that saying that it would help Frank think about thinking, whatever that means. He was planning his next science project in his head when the bus suddenly stopped. Andy woke up and looked at Frank. "Why did we stop?" Andy asked while rubbing his eyes, "This is not our stop, is it?"

"No," replied Frank. Then, the doors crashed open and two men with guns climbed aboard the bus. Frank and Andy realized what was going on. They looked at each other in panic. Everyone on the bus were screaming.

"Oh, come on! They are robbing us! What are we going to do now?" Andy asked.

"What in the world! Should we hide?" asked Frank.

They looked around and they did not see anywhere to hide, the bus was full. *Think Frank, think!* Frank thought. He was trying to find a way to leave that bus safely and quickly, as two guys were yelling at the driver. The driver raised his hands and begged them not to hurt him. One of the bad guys was tall and muscular. His long black hair was in a ponytail down his neck. The other one was shorter and skinnier, with short brown hair.

"I'll watch them with the gun while you are working, go!" said the muscular bad guy. "Everybody! QUIET!" His voice almost shook the bus. "We don't want to harm you. We just need your valuables. If you cooperate, nobody gets hurt."

The skinnier guy was looking at him confused.

"Why are you looking at me?! Go collect their stuff!" the muscular one shouted.

"OK Greg," the shorter guy responded.

"How many times should I tell you not to use my name when we are doing business, you stupid!" His mouth spitted out foams when he spoke.

"I'm sorry Greg…Oops, I did it again, didn't I? So sorry…"

Andy whispered to Frank, "One of them looks dumb, the other one is the leader for sure."

"How do you know? And why do we care?"

"The dumb one always looks at his partner whenever there is a decision to be made. He does what the other one asks him to do."

"OK. Thanks for the analysis, Sherlock, but this is not something we can use here to escape, Andy!"

The bossy one repeated, "Everybody stays still! We just want your money, that's it, nobody has to get hurt! Just cooperate!" He turned to his dumb partner. "Quick!"

Frank and Andy sat right by the door in the back of the bus.

Andy said in fear, "They will take my watches and my money from me. Then what am I going to tell my mom? Oh, they will take your tablet too! We are so much in trouble!"

Frank was not listening to Andy; at that moment, he was looking around and trying to find something that could help them escape. Then he saw the trees outside. If they could open the back door, they both could run into the woods in about ten seconds.

"We can run to the woods," said Frank.

"Wait, *those* woods? No way!"

Andy was now making Frank upset. "Why not? We could hide there for a while until we get on a new bus or something."

"You don't know, Frank. It is dangerous down there in the forest…" his voice was thick with fear.

"Look, we don't know who these men are. They might be crazy and kill us all!" Frank said.

"You're right." Andy had a moment of enlightenment. "They are not even wearing masks."

"What does that mean?"

"It means they are not afraid of being seen or recognized later. Because…Because they are going to kill us all!" Andy yelled.

The two men glared at them.

"Calm down Andy, don't be an idiot," Frank whispered and nervously smiled at the men. The dumb one was collecting all the jewelry, money and electronics from the passengers. Everyone was so frightened that some people had passed out. The two high school girls sitting in front of Frank and Andy were crying non-stop. This old grandma across the aisle was praying constantly with her cross necklace in her hand. The dumb one was half way finished already, they were getting closer to the back door, where Andy and Frank were seated.

"I don't know about your universe, but in my world, woods are extremely dangerous, Frank."

"More dangerous than two men with guns?"

Andy hesitated, "…Could be!" He hunched and started biting his nails.

"Listen, we need to try. We don't have any other choice right now and we need to act quickly. I want you to focus on our escape now. We will deal with the woods later, if we are lucky."

"OK." Andy nodded nervously.

"How can we open this door?" asked Frank.

"Umm…There are two ways. You push this button and the driver opens the door at the stop. The second one is the emergency lever."

"Perfect! Where is that?"

"There, above the door," Andy pointed.

"It is too high. I will need to get on your shoulders."

"Oh man, this already sounds so stupidly dangerous!" said Andy trembling.

The dumb one now was five seats away. Frank couldn't hide his frustration anymore. "Andy, we need to do this now or we will die. How does this thing work? It looks like it has an arm."

"Yea, I never tried before but I guess you pull that thing down," Andy said.

"You are not sure? Great!" Frank was trying to calm down. "OK. Here is the plan. You get up quietly, and I will climb on your shoulders. I'll pull down the arm as fast as I can, and as soon as the door opens, we will run into the woods straight, without looking back, alright? Do not look back, ever. Do you understand?"

"Got it." said Andy.

Frank was trying to hide the fact that he was scared. But he could hear his heart pounding. His hands were so sweaty that he wasn't even sure if he could grab the lever without slipping. How he wished he was in his Aurora Shell right now! He took a deep breath and said, "On the count of three."

Andy nodded.

"1...2...3!"

Andy quickly but quietly managed to walk in front of the door without being seen. The dumb one was busy emptying the pockets of the passengers, and the boss one was looking the other way. Frank quickly jumped on Andy and climbed on both his shoulders. He reached out to the small red arm. He grabbed it and pulled it down with his own weight. The door opened with a big hiss. It was so loud that everybody now was looking at them.

Frank yelled at Andy, "GO!"

They both jumped out of the bus and started running for their lives. As they ran, Frank heard the boss one yelling, "Stop them!" He ran as fast as he could. *Why does ten seconds feel like ten hours already?* he thought. Then he was almost to the woods. He couldn't see Andy next to him, couldn't hear him either. He was worried about his friend. It was when he entered the woods that he heard the sound of the rifle. He heard multiple shots.

"Andy!" Frank now was more worried than ever. He talked to himself, "I hope you are OK, my friend. Oh God, I hope you are OK!"

After five minutes of nonstop running deep into the woods, he finally had the courage to stop and look around. It was so quiet. He could just hear birds chirping. That was it. Frank tried to catch his breath.

"Andy!" he yelled into the woods. It echoed. "Where are you?"

No response. Just leaves rustling in the wind.

Frank was getting more and more worried. He had a terrible feeling that his friend might have been hurt, or worse, gone. That was when suddenly he heard someone running toward him. But this person was running really slowly. Frank wasn't sure if it was Andy or one of the bad men. He quickly hid behind the trunk of a large tree and tried to see who it was. The person stopped running and started walking instead.

"Frank?" the tired voice called.

"Andy?!" Frank came out of his hiding place and looked at Andy. "You are alive!"

"Well, I guess so." He smiled and rested his hands on his knees to catch his breath.

Frank jumped out of the bushes and ran to his friend. He gave him a long hug. "It's OK Andy. We made it."

Andy patted Frank's back. He was still having trouble catching his breath. "Yes, we did!"

Frank finally let Andy go and gave him a high five.

"I don't get why you are scared of these woods, Andy. Looks pretty calm and nice so far."

"Let's just say I have heard stories." Andy started to follow Frank, as they walked down the path through thick woods. The path was beautiful, flanked by tall, leafy trees on both sides with healthy colored trunks, thick branches growing out every direction, with dense leaves dancing in the breeze. Each one of them smelled different. One smelled like orange. After walking for a while, they could smell something like a mixture of pine and cinnamon.

"What stories?" Frank asked curiously. Then took a deep breath, inhaling all the nice smells at once. The smell of orange reminded him of the jam his mom used to make. *How much I miss Mom,* he thought.

Andy kicked the pebbles that got in his way while walking. "Well, we have certain animals that live in the woods that are really dangerous. They are big meat eaters."

"Carnivores."

"Whatever. Like us, you know. The only difference is we are their steak."

Frank corrected Andy. "But we are omnivores."

"What is the difference?"

"Omnivores eat both plants and meat. Carnivores only eat meat."

"Oh, I see. Anyway. They are giant and dangerous, some of them are really fast, too. They live freely in the woods."

"Do you mean like bears or tigers?"

"We also have those in woods but I'm talking about Konggongs."

"Do you mean King Kong?" Frank laughed but Andy was clueless.

"No, friend. The apartment-high, egg laying, meat eating, scary animals that I'm talking about."

"What you are describing sounds like dinosaurs. But they disappeared millions of years ago!" Frank suddenly stopped. "Wait a minute…Are you saying that the meteorite never hit the earth in this universe and dinosaurs live among us?"

"You are not making any sense right now. Sorry, Frank. I don't know what dinosore is and when this meteorite thingy hit the world but Konggongs are real, and if they sound similar to dinosore then you can call them that, I'm fine with it."

"Dinosaur! Not Dinosore." Frank was amused one more time about this universe. "So cool! Konggongs, huh? I would love to see one! So, it is like *Jurassic Park* here. Wow, who would have thought!"

"What is *Jurassic Park*?"

"An awesome movie. They keep dinosaurs...I mean Konggongs in a gigantic park, and these animals suddenly cut loose and start to eat people in the park!"

"Very encouraging, Thanks!" Andy checked his back and surroundings nervously. Drops of sweat were making his forehead look shiny. "What happens in the end of the movie?"

"Oh well, you know. Some people die."

"Lovely!" said Andy, looking around even more scared now. "Where are we going anyway?"

"Well, we will follow the direction of the highway for an hour or so and see if there are other stops on the way. Once we find one, we can hop on the next bus and head home," Frank said confidently.

"What do you think happened to the passengers back there?" Andy asked in a sad voice.

"I don't know, really. I hope they all made it safe."

"Yeah." Andy took a deep breath. "I hope so too...I heard gunshots, though."

"Yeah, I heard them too. I hope they are OK. Well, I'm glad you're OK." Frank smiled.

The beauty of the woods was breathtaking. The air was so fresh, the colors of the trees and flowers were so bright, and the smell of the soil was incredibly refreshing. Frank saw many different kinds of flowers and plants he had never seen. Some of them were moving, like alive, just like the ivy he saw on the way. Some of them had giant neon blue and yellow flowers as big as a dishwasher. Frank was really enjoying this hike. But they were getting tired and hungry; they had been walking for a little over an hour now. Along the way, they talked about sports, science and the horror stories about Konggongs. Frank was worried about these animals, but he didn't want Andy to know. He was trying to look cool so he didn't freak him out more.

"It is going to get dark soon, Frank," Andy said.

"Yeah I know. Let's give it a try."

They walked up to hill leading to the highway. It was surprisingly quiet and there were no bus stops nearby.

"This is not good," Frank said to himself. "Maybe we should stop a car?"

"Two 11-year-old boys hitchhiking doesn't sound safe."

"Yes, but sleeping with Konggongs overnight doesn't sound safe, either." Frank replied.

"Good point." Andy checked the both directions of the highway. "Let's wait a little, maybe we could stop a bus or police car?"

"It is worth a try!" Andy said.

They sat by the highway for thirty minutes or so. There were no cars passing and no luck with any buses, either.

"This is strange," Andy said.

"They might have closed the road because of the robbery," Frank said.

"Oh, no!" Andy cried. He opened his hands both sides, palms up. "What are we going to do now?"

Losing their hope for the day, they went back in the woods and continued walking on the path. They decided to look around to find a safe place to spend the night.

"Did you hear that?!" said Andy in fear.

"Hear what?"

"Shh!" Andy hushed Frank and they listened.

Crack.

"Someone is there!" Frank whispered to Andy.

Hearing someone approaching, they quickly hid in the nearest bushes. A relatively big in size, odd looking animal came along. It looked like an ostrich but had shorter legs and a shorter neck. It had a thick, long, hairy tail as well. Frank had never seen this type of animal before. It was sniffing the trees, looking behind the bushes and digging in the soil as if it was trying to find some food.

"I have never seen that animal before," Frank whispered.

"It's a kind of Konggong, they are smaller. I think they're called iklas. This one is small so I assume it is a baby one."

"It doesn't look that small to me…Are they dangerous?" asked Frank in fear.

"Well they are carbibores."

"Carnivore," corrected Frank.

"That one," smiled Andy.

Suddenly, something unexpected happened. The ikla turned its face towards Frank and Andy's hiding place and started to walk toward them slowly.

Both Andy and Frank were frozen with fear.

"Oops! Do you think it has noticed us? What are we going to do?" asked Andy.

"I don't know. They say don't run from bears. No idea about iklas!"

A few feet away from the bushes, the ikla stopped. It tilted its head as if it was trying to hear something. Then, it growled and hissed, directly looking at the two.

Andy said, "I don't like this at all Frank. We are so in trouble!" his voice was shaking.

"Run!" Frank yelled.

Once again, they were running through the woods. But this time their enemy was way faster than them. Andy and Frank could hear the ikla getting closer.

"I'm too young to die Frank!" yelled Andy.

Frank couldn't even respond because he was trying to breathe. Frank could hear the ikla taking giant leaps just behind him while running. For a second, he wondered if it could also fly. A painful squeak instantly echoed in the forest, followed by a loud rumble. The ikla must have fallen down because it wasn't following them anymore. Frank stopped running. "Andy, stop! I think it is gone!"

Andy threw himself on his knees and looked back at Frank, trying to catch his breath. "It was too close, Frank!" They both were panting. "Should we look?" Frank asked. Andy shook his head as if saying, *hell no*. But Frank's curiosity was overpowering. He found himself walking towards the lifeless body of ikla which was lying on the ground peacefully. Not wanting to stand there alone, Andy joined his friend involuntarily.

Andy said, "Look!" he pointed at an arrow that had struck the ikla in its right thigh. "Someone killed the thing."

Frank looked down and saw the small arrow. "What in the world?"

They both heard a branch cracked up in a nearby tree, breaking the silence. When they looked up where the sound came from, a girl was smiling at them from the top. Stood on a thick branch, with one hand she was holding onto the trunk and carrying a bow with the other. "Hey boys, what's up?"

"You killed it!" Andy yelled at her.

"Well, is that how you thank someone who saved your lives?" said the girl. She climbed down the tree in a matter of seconds and walked closer to them. "Besides, it is not dead. Just sleeping for now. But in ten minutes or so it will wake up. I suggest we get going. Shall we?"

Andy and Frank looked at each other, puzzled. Frank fixed his glasses and couldn't help but ask, "Excuse me, umm...We don't even know your name, or who you are. Why would we follow you?"

Andy interrupted. "Thank you by the way, for saving our lives. But please understand, we don't know you."

Her weird clothes caught Andy's attention. Well, if you could call them clothes. She had worn, dirty, knee-high boots and had a knee-length burlap sack on, which had minor holes in it. Over the sack, a belt from the same material was wrapped around her waist. Her long black hair was messy but clean. *She must be our age*, thought Frank.

"You are more polite than your friend," said the girl to Andy. "My name is Ada."

"What are you doing here, Ada?" asked Frank.

"I should ask the same question to you." She put her bow in her belt. "I live here. Never seen you around before. Are you lost?"

"A very long story," said Andy. "We were looking for a safe place to stay tonight."

Frank poked Andy with his elbow and Andy responded, "What? I trust her, she saved our lives."

The ikla groaned and whined.

"Look, Frank! It is not dead!" Andy said. "Just like she said!"

"It is waking up. We need to go quickly! Move!" said Ada.

Being both impressed and afraid of her, they did their best to follow Ada. She was so fast. One minute she was jumping, rolling, and the other she was crawling along the river bed. *Is she in military?* Frank thought for a second. They certainly were having a hard time keeping up with her. Once they got to the safe distance, she started talking again.

"OK. We are safe now." She slowed down her walking pace. "So, what are your names and what is your story?"

Frank was impatient. "Could you just tell us where we are going first?"

Andy interrupted, "Sorry, we have been walking and running around a lot today. Also, we are really tired. My name is Andy, and this is my friend Frank."

"Nice to meet you Andy and grumpy Frank!" Ada smiled.

"I'm not grumpy!" Frank turned to Andy and said, "Can you believe she called me grumpy? I don't like being called by names."

Ada laughed. "Relax, I'm taking you to my village. You can spend the night at my house. It is safe there, trust me."

Frank wasn't sure about who to trust anymore. He realized that the world was a dangerous place and people could lie very easily these days. But he also trusted Andy's judgment. *If Andy trusts her, she must be reliable,* he thought.

The night had already fallen, and they were still walking.

"Andy, do you know anything about these forest villages? Because you seem really comfortable about following her. You are the suspicious one usually," Frank whispered.

"Not much. Everyone talks about them as a myth. I can't believe they are real! It's been said they are the bravest people you can ever meet. I mean, they live among Konggongs!" Andy whispered back.

Frank wasn't that convinced yet. "What were you doing this far away from your village?" Frank asked suspiciously.

"Your friend has trust issues, Andy," said Ada, "I was training. Children at my age usually don't start hunting yet. But I want to make my mama and papa proud, you know?"

As she finished her sentence a flock of birds took off of a nearby tree. Frank noticed it, but she didn't see it. She continued talking. "I had been following that ikla for an hour or so before I caught him. They become vulnerable when they feed. I was waiting for the right moment. When you..." The ground shook with a deep rumble, not letting Ada finish her sentence. Then it shook again. It was such a strong rumble that Frank lost his balance and almost fell. The sound came from afar but the intensity of shake was increasing by the minute. Whatever thing was making this noise was approaching, fast. "This is not good, we need to hurry!" said Ada, her eyes wide open. "Follow me, this way!" They ran to this wide, fast and turbulent river, where the only bridge was a long log stretching from one side to the other. Ada hopped up and started walking across it. She opened her both arms to keep her balance. In the middle of the river she paused as she realized they were not following her anymore. "What is wrong?"

Andy and Frank looked at each other then looked at the log. Andy shook his head.

"Oh, come on! It is so easy. Just open your arms and focus on your feet." Ada yelled. The sound of turbulent water was muffling her words.

"Easier said than done!" said Frank dryly.

Andy went first. Then Frank followed his friend. Both of them finally managed to cross the river although it took them twice as long as it had taken Ada. She definitely had a lot of fun watching them sweat. "We made it!! On this side of the river, we are safe from Konggongs." She said joyfully. "Don't worry, my village is really close!"

After a short and sweet walk along the river, they arrived in a valley, surrounded by red-colored mountain ranges. The village had many clay houses encircled by brown fences. It looked very pretty from where Frank stood. *She was right*, Frank thought to himself. He felt bad that he had been so suspicious of her since the beginning.

They walked down the hill and halfway into the village. There were a few people around looking at them, as if they were aliens. Realizing that this could be uncomfortable for them, Ada told Andy and Frank, "They are not used to strangers. Don't worry, as long as you are with me, you are fine."

All the clay houses had only one story, and they were relatively small with a low ceiling. Inside the fences, Andy could see some animals sleeping or feeding. He couldn't see what kind,

though, since the village was too dark. There was a barbecue-like smell in the air, reminding Frank how hungry he was.

Finally, they stopped in front of a clay house with a pretty door made of bamboo leaves. There were sacks at the windows taking the place of curtains. Due to the fear of unknown, both Andy and Frank were reluctant to enter the house.

Ada looked at them, surprised. "What happened to you guys? You are scared of everything. Can't wait to hear your story." She half-opened the bamboo leaves. "Come on in! This is my house."

The bamboo leaves opened into a cozy medium-size living room. There were thick bamboo rugs and some old, colorful pillows lying around everywhere. The only light source was the fire place in the middle of the room and some candles lighting up the narrow hall way. A sauce pan was placed near the fire and something was steaming inside. Whatever it was, it smelled really good.

"Hungry?" asked Ada.

"Hell yes!" replied Andy and just sat right next to the fire. He looked into the pan. "What is this?"

"It is my mom's specialty: Ikla stew."

"I guess you are not hungry?" Ada asked Frank.

"Hmm…Smells delicious!" said Andy, Frank was still standing by the door, looking at the house. A bookcase carved from a tree trunk in the corner caught his attention. He started walking that way.

"Oh, I'm starving," Frank replied. "Who reads these?" He grabbed one of the books from the bookshelf and started looking inside.

"My dad. I read some of them too," said Ada.

"These are about galaxies, atoms and human anatomy." Frank was checking out the cover of the books. He seemed surprised. "What does your dad do?"

"He does what the others do here. We all hunt. But he is also the healer of our community. He collects herbs and other plants to make his own medicine."

"Wow, cool!" Frank put the book back on the oak shelf. "So, where are your parents?"

"They both went hunting together with some villagers. I don't think they will be back until tomorrow," Ada said.

"It does smell yummy in here. Can I have some of that stew, too?" Frank asked.

"Of course, help yourself!" Ada replied.

For an hour or so, the only thing they did was talk and eat. Ada couldn't believe her ears when she heard about the bus robbery. She was also very impressed by the fact that Andy and Frank were able to find their way back by using a simple watch.

"So...what is your story Ada?" asked Andy. "Who are your people? Why do you live here?"

"Apparently, once upon a time, we used to live in the city. But the food got worse, they started to use a lot of chemicals in them. People got really competitive and ugly at work and in politics. It was really hard to get a job or keep a job. The economy was not doing well. People were missing nature and natural things. So, a small group of people decided to build their own community in the middle of the woods. In the beginning, I guess there were like twenty or thirty people. Now there are about four hundred of us. We still get out of the woods time to time. My dad collects books from the dump sites. I go by the lake and play with the kids there sometimes. But I like to be here. It is safe and healthy. I feel happy here."

"How about Konggongs? Aren't you scared that they could come here and eat you up?" Andy asked, nervously.

"For some reason, they can't cross that river. The one you were scared to pass. Apparently, they are scared too. That is why they built our village here. We are surrounded by the river."

"Well let's hope the sea level will never fall around here," Frank murmured.

"Do you ever want to go to school? Or go to restaurants, movies, game parks?" Andy said.

"We have a school here. It is the last clay building to the north. We cook together and eat together when the weather is nice. We play games sometimes, make jokes, tell stories by the fire. We are really having a good time here. Actually, I should ask you, my friends. You work for other people in those stores and restaurants. Yet, they don't pay you much and you look unhappy all the time. Have you ever thought about quitting and starting your own world or system from scratch?"

"All the time!" said Andy. "For some reason, your life sounds way cooler than my life right now."

They all laughed, ate and talked that night. Ada prepared the guest room for them. Having been running and walking around all day, they fell asleep as soon as they hit the pillows. The pillows were so soft and they smelled like pine trees. Probably they both had the best sleep of their lives that night.

When they woke up really early the next morning, they found some boiled eggs by the fire with a note saying, "Sorry I had to leave early for training. Just keep heading west from here, you will find the highway. Be careful Andy and Mr. Grumpy! PS. Eggs are fresh."

"Can't believe she leaves this early, wow," said Andy.

"Do you think these are ikla eggs?" Frank asked.

"I have no idea!" said Andy and took a bite. "Whatever they are, they are delicious."

After finishing their eggs, they headed back to the highway, using the golden watch as their compass. This time they were determined to either find the bus stop or get a ride in a police car. They were sure that they didn't want to spend one more night in now what they called "iklaland."

Walking by the road, they attracted a lot of attention. The highway traffic seemed normal today. *They must have opened the roads*, Frank thought. Some cars slowed down with an unknown intention, but Andy gave the OK sign to show them they were not interested. About a half-hour later, they saw a police car chasing another car in the distance. They started waving at the police car. They jumped and down, holding their backpacks in their hands. But the police car drove past them so fast that probably they didn't even see Frank and Andy.

"Zazingo!" said Andy, kicked a pebble by the road, frustrated. He sat down by the road. "We will never get out of here!"

Frank yelled behind him. "Wait a minute...Andy! They stopped!" He pointed in the direction of the cars. The police car had pulled up by the side of the road and the police officer slowly got out of the car. He was looking Frank and Andy's way.

"He is waving at us! He saw us Andy! We are going home!"

Andy and Frank started running towards the police car. As they approached the car, their hearts were filled with joy. They were not going to sleep in the woods tonight.

"Hello boys. What are you doing up here all by yourselves? Where are your parents?" He was sizing them both up as he spoke.

Andy said, "There was a robbery on a bus and we had to run away. Could you please take us home?"

"Good grief! Were you on that bus? You are so lucky you made it out of there." He opened the passenger door of the police car in shock. "Get in the car. Just give me the address and I will drop you off."

"26 Park Avenue," said Andy.

"How about you, child?" the policeman asked Frank.

Before even Frank could open his mouth, Andy answered, "We're brothers. We're going to the same address."

"That's great." He started the engine. "Did you guys put on your seat belts back there?"

"Yes sir!" said Andy and winked at Frank.

During the ride, Frank thought this was the first time he had actually been in a police car. In movies, the police cars looked cooler than this. There was a lot of trash on the passenger seat and on the floor. It smelled like something between fries and sweat. The police radio was cool though. You could hear every call they made.

"The bus you escaped from. Nobody else made it out of there alive. Your parents must be losing their minds right now," said the officer.

Both Frank and Andy looked at each other. They were terrified at the news but also felt so lucky to have made it out of there alive.

After a long ride, they arrived at Andy's place. The kind police officer walked both of them to the house and wanted to talk to Andy's mom. Andy was worried that his mom was going to get really mad at him in front of the police officer and Frank. But luckily, nobody answered the door.

"It's OK, I have the keys," said Andy. He took out his keys and opened the door. The police officer smiled and said, "I don't want to see you anywhere near the highway again OK boys? Not until you're at least 16."

They both nodded.

"Yes, sir," said Andy.

"This is my phone number and name. Please give it to your parents and tell them to give me a call once they come home. Otherwise, I will come tonight to check up on you both."

"Will do!" Andy smiled.

Frank somehow knew that Andy's mom would never call this officer.

They watched the police officer get in his car and leave. When they got inside the house, Andy checked everywhere. His mom wasn't home. He locked the door and sat on the stairway.

"Where is your mom do you think?" Frank asked.

"This is normally her nap hour. Her not being here is definitely not a good sign. But I will handle it, like always. Don't worry about me," Andy smiled.

"Thank you for everything Andy. You were right…Without you, I wouldn't have been able to survive out there."

"No problem, friend. It was fun," Andy winked. They both laughed. This winking thing had become their thing now.

They went upstairs. Frank changed back to his own clothes. Then, he took down the Big Bang poster slowly. He threw his backpack into the wormhole first, then he climbed in. He looked at his friend one more time. He could see how worried he was and he felt so sad that there was nothing he could do for him.

"What are you going to do now?" Frank asked.

"Probably walk to downtown and try to sell that watch first. Let's see if that will be enough to make my mother happy," Andy shrugged.

"See you tomorrow?" Frank asked.

"Hope so, Frank! I have nothing planned so far," Andy smiled.

But as Frank was crawling through the wormhole towards his Aurora Shell, he didn't know that he wouldn't be able to see his friend for a while.

10

FAMILY

After their short but adventurous journey, everything changed for Frank. As soon as he arrived back in his room, he didn't even wait for the morning. He ran straight to his parents' bedroom where he found them sleeping. He climbed up into their bed and held them so tight.

"What's wrong Frankie?" Joe checked the time. It was the middle of the night.

Francine was awake too. "Sweetie, you are a little too old to sleep with us in the bed, don't you think?" She smiled and gave him a kiss on the forehead.

"Mom, Dad…I love you…Thank you for being who you are!" Frank said.

Both Francine and Joe were confused at this random confession of love.

"Oh…Frank, you know your father and I love you so, so much. We were actually talking about this yesterday."

She sat up in the bed, and Frank's dad did the same.

Francine continued, "We realized that recently we haven't been there for you as much as we should have. You've probably realized, we are having some problems these days…I mean, money-related problems, but it will all be over soon and we are so sorry we reflected this on you." She gently stroked Frank's hair as she talked.

Joe continued where Francine left off. "We care about you a lot and we want to give you a perfect future. That is why we were stressed…But I have some good news!" Frank thought he had never seen these many teeth in his dad's mouth. His smile was that big.

"What is it?" asked Frank impatiently.

Francine yelled in joy, "Dad got a new job!"

This was the best news ever for Frank. It meant things would likely go back to they were in the good old days when both of his parents were happy and had time to spend with him. "Yay!" Frank jumped on the bed. "That's awesome!" for a second, he couldn't help but think, *Maybe I might get that red telescope now!* His parents were laughing together with him.

Frank thought that this journey to the other side had taught him a lot. He had learned that happiness doesn't mean one thing. Edward had his birth parents by his side, but he wasn't happy.

Andy didn't have the best parents, but he was happy with Frank and with his cat, Love. Ada didn't live in a big expensive house and worked every day, but she was happier than any other kid in Frank's neighborhood. Then he thought, *I'm adopted…So, what? I've the best parents I could ask for who love me more than anything, I have a great friend who is always honest with me and who is funny. I have my Aurora Shell, my science books, my Star Wars series. I'm literally the luckiest kid in the universe. Well, maybe in all universes!*

That night, Frank had a dream. In his dream they were in a different house. 'Love' the cat woke him up in the morning licking his face. Then when he went downstairs to have breakfast, he saw Andy sitting at the table, eating cereal. "Good morning Frank!"

"Good morning sleepyhead. Your brother woke up earlier than you did this time," said Joe, making eggs by the stove.

"My brother?" Frank suddenly felt this joy filling up his body from his head to toe. "My brother!"

Frank ran downstairs and gave a big hug to Andy, so tight that Andy almost fell off his chair.

"Good morning Frankie" said his mother. But for some reason, even though she was very close to Frank, she sounded far away.

"School time, you are going to be late. Wake up sweetie!" Now her voice was getting closer and closer.

"*Frank?*"

Frank slowly opened his eyes to see a blurry image of his mom.

"Mom?"

"Were you expecting someone else?" she smiled.

"No, it's just. My dream was...super real."

"Oh, really? Was it a good dream?" She got up and picked up his dirty laundry bag from the corner of the room.

"Yes" Frank stretched and yawned. "It was too good to be true."

"Come on now, get ready. Your dad is leaving early. Remember, this is his first day at his new job. He will drop you off at school first, then he will go to work."

"OK. I will be downstairs in five."

"Thank you!" Francine blew a kiss and left the room with the laundry bag.

Frank was upset that his dream was just a dream. He couldn't wait to see Andy in the evening. They had never had the chance to talk about the ikla and Ada. Also, Frank wanted to know how Andy's mom reacted when she found out what happened. He hoped that she hadn't gotten too mad at him.

That day, Frank crushed it at school. He got an A+ on his latest math test. During the lunch break, he met two kids that he had never met before and was actually able to have a good conversation without making anybody annoyed. Andy would have been proud of him. Then, his science teacher asked him to join a team for this special science project. Only five people were chosen from the whole school and he was one of them, the only one from his grade. His parents were going to be so happy and proud.

Francine showed up fifteen minutes late to pick him up, but nothing could make him upset that day. It was OK. It was such a lovely day. The sun was shining although the weather was still cold, people were walking, chatting and laughing in the streets, birds were singing as if spring was already here. Frank watched the people in the coffee shop across the street. The place was packed. By the window, he saw two men showing something to each other on their phones and smiling. *They must be good friends,* he thought. *Just like Andy and I.*

As soon as his mom arrived, he opened the back door of the car and threw in his backpack.

"Hey honey, how was school?" Francine asked.

Frank climbed into the car, closed the door and started talking about his day nonstop. "You won't believe what happened today mom. So, in Math class, Mr. O'Malley–"

His mom had to remind him to put on his seatbelt because he was so excited about everything that had happened. Frank quickly did so then kept going on about how awesome his day was. During the ride home, his mom kept saying, "Good job Frankie!" "Oh, that's my boy!" "I'm so proud of you buddy!" and that made him feel proud and special.

Frank thought, *this is a wonderful day.* But he was going to feel that way until it was the night time.

Andy hadn't visited yet. Frank wanted to check up on him but wasn't sure if it was the right time to go and see him. What if Andy's mom saw him? This would make everything so difficult for Andy. *He will eventually come by,* Frank thought.

Three days passed. The absence of Andy worried Frank. This wasn't normal, something was wrong. He decided to check up on Andy at midnight.

After he made sure his parents were sleeping, he crawled down the wormhole. He thought about what to tell Andy when he saw him. He was going to tell him about the two kids he met and about the science project group he was in. Actually, Frank needed Andy's opinion for that.

Finally, he got to the Big Bang poster on Andy's side of the wormhole. "Andy?" Frank whispered through the thin paper.

No response.

"Andy, are you there?"

Silence.

He couldn't even hear Love. He decided he had to see what was going on, despite the risk of Andy's mom being there. He slowly started to take down the poster from inside. He made a little tear on the upper left corner. *Oops! He is going to kill me,* he thought.

When he jumped into the room, he saw that everything was untouched. The bed was made, the PC was off. No cookies, no open books…No signs of Andy.

This is strange, Frank thought, *something feels wrong.*

He decided to check the house. If Andy were there to hear this idea, he would definitely not like it. But Frank had to make sure that his friend was alright. He turned the door knob and nothing happened. It was locked from outside!

"What?" Frank was confused. *Why?* he thought. He put his ear to the door and tried to listen into the hallway, tried to hear anything, but it was dead quiet.

Maybe they left town for a few days, he guessed, *he should be back soon.*

With these confusing thoughts in his mind, he crawled back to his Aurora Shell. He tried to read about continental drift that night, which he always found super interesting. But he couldn't concentrate. He would read one page then realize that he didn't understand more than half of what he had just read because he was thinking about Andy. He put his tablet away and turned on the LED light. Like he did every time he felt worried or upset, he watched the northern lights dancing.

"He is OK," he said to calm himself down. But for some reason, he couldn't believe what he just said.

Something wasn't right.

Mr. and Mrs. Gallagher were over for dinner on this snowy and cold Saturday night. *Why would they even leave their homes in this weather?* Frank wondered. The adults were talking about boring stuff like work, politicians, babies and fashion.

I wish the Gallaghers had a kid, Frank thought, *we could play computer games or something.*

He never liked guests very much. They were loud and most of the time they were fake when they were talking to him. "Oh, look at him, he's grown up so much!" "How old are you now?" "Do you like your school?" "What do you want to be when you grow up?" The problem was, the minute they walked out the door, they would forget the answers to their questions. It was just waste of everybody's time, especially Frank's. He didn't like any neighbors except the neighbor boy Ramzi, and the neighbor across the street, Ms. Hilltop. She was so smart. She was a professor at the university in town, and she taught geology. So, each time she came, she would bring a science set and they would set it up together. One time she brought a fossil collection. Frank's jaw had dropped when he saw it. He literally slept with his 450 million-year-old trilobite for two weeks.

"What is wrong Frankie? You haven't been eating well lately. Are you feeling sick?" Francine looked at him really worried. She was putting the dishes away while Joe and Gallaghers were playing a board game.

It had been two weeks since he last saw Andy. He was not going to tell his mother that.

"Can I go up to my room? I'm not feeling well," Frank said.

"How about I make you some warm chocolate milk?"

"Thanks Mom, but I don't want it."

"Honey, I'm worried about you…You didn't eat anything today." She put her hand on his forehead and tried to feel his temperature. "Thank God, you don't have a fever. OK. So, I will let you go upstairs and get some rest but I also want you to promise me to eat." She grabbed some goldfish crackers from the top of the fridge and gave them to Frank. "When I come upstairs to check up on you, I want to see an empty bag of goldfish. Do you understand?"

Frank nodded.

"Good boy!" She gave him a kiss. "I will be up later to check up on you, OK?"

"OK."

On the way upstairs, he thought about a plan to see Andy. He closed his door, walked towards his PC and sat on the chair in the dark quietly for a while. A few minutes later, a decision had just been made; *Tonight, I will visit Andy's house again.*

If anyone could see his search history on the Internet, he would definitely be in trouble. Researching how to open locked doors without using a key would make him seem like a criminal. He was actually shocked to find so much information about it so easily online. Soon, there were plan A, B and C. Plan A was to use a credit card to open the door. Well, he was going to use his student ID card, which was practically the same thing. Plan B was using a paper clip. Plan C was a coat hanger. The demonstrations were all on the Internet with step by step videos. He packed his backpack with what he needed and waited for his parents to go to bed.

The Gallaghers stayed annoyingly late that night. After the guests left, his mother came by and gave him a kiss. He pretended to be asleep. As soon as his parents went to bed, he grabbed his backpack and crawled into the wormhole. He got into Andy's room, taped the poster back, then slowly approached the door. He tried to open it again, just in case, but it was still locked. "OK. Here we go," Frank said and tried to open the door with his school ID. *Nah, the card's too thin!* he thought, *plan B then.* He did his best to open the door with the paper clips. He ruined the first two paper clips and fished in his backpack for a third.

This looked way easier in the video! he thought.

After minutes of effort, he heard, *"Click!"*

He was finally out. Nobody was in the hallway. He walked down the hall and checked Andy's mother's room first. She was sleeping in her bed. There was a gin bottle knocked over on the carpet and cigarette ashes everywhere.

Andy, where are you my friend? Frank thought.

He went downstairs, checked the living room and kitchen. Everything was such a mess. There were dirty clothes on the couch, there was a thick layer of dust on the TV, and more on the carpet. Love must have knocked over things, because there was broken glass everywhere. The dishes hadn't been done for a while, and all the food on the counters and the unwashed plates was rotten. Fruit flies were everywhere.

It doesn't look like Andy has been around for a while. He would have cleaned this mess up! Frank thought, *where is he?*

The more he walked around, the more worried Frank felt. He went upstairs and checked on Andy's mother again. She was still asleep. Then he decided to check the other part of the hallway where there was only an empty room and a bathroom. *What do I have to lose?* he thought.

As he was walking towards the bathroom upstairs, Frank heard Love.

"Meow!"

Frank wasn't sure where exactly the sound was coming from.

"Love?" Frank called her name, whispering, "Love, where are you?"

"Meow! Meow!"

It was coming from Andy's brother's room. Frank tried to get in the room but it was locked.

This doesn't make sense! Frank thought, *why would Love be locked in here?*

"Frank?" came a very familiar but also weak voice from beyond the door.

Frank's heart jumped. "Andy!" Frank tried to whisper back to him through the solid wood, "Is that you in there?"

"Help me!" Andy cried.

Frank grabbed the remaining paper clips from his backpack and started to work on the lock. But Love was making too much noise, she was getting impatient.

"Andy! Make Love calm down please. She is going to wake up your mother!"

A few seconds later, Love was totally silent, and with that Frank could concentrate better.

"Shut up for God's sake!" Andy's mother groaned from her room.

Frank's heart pounded so hard that he thought his chest would split in two. It was too late. She was already awake. Frank prayed as hard as he could that she wouldn't get up until he opened the door. He was working on the lock with two clips now. He kept one steady and kept turning the other. But it was losing grip so easily. He tried again, failed again. Tried one more time. Failed again. He was sweating like crazy. Now his hands were slippery as well. He wiped his hands on his jeans and tried again.

Click!

Frank quickly opened the door, went into the dark room and closed the door quietly. The first thing Frank noticed was the strong odor of cat pee. Then he felt Love snuggling between his legs as if she was thanking him. When Frank looked at the other side of the room, he saw Andy. He had lost so much weight. He looked so weak and unhealthy. He looked so different that Frank thought for a second that this might not be Andy. But it was him. It was so dark inside that he wanted to turn on the light but then he also didn't want Andy's mother to know. He opened the curtains but it didn't help much because the window was facing a brick wall. But at least he could see his friend's face more clearly now.

"What happened to you?" Frank asked. He was terrified.

Andy had a black eye. His lips were so dry that they were bleeding. He was dirty and he had some cuts and big bruises on his arms and legs. He was in really bad shape which broke Frank's heart so deeply.

"My mom got so angry after we got back…" Andy was so weak that he could barely talk. "The watch money didn't work. She didn't believe my story. She started throwing things at me. I was hiding in the living room." He gulped. "I was waiting…I was waiting for her to fall asleep or get tired you know? But she didn't. She was so mad that she locked me up here with Love. I've been here since we came back. She gives me food and water once a day, which I share with Love." He started crying. "She says that she wished that I had died instead of Mike."

Frank hugged his friend and let him cry on his shoulder. But they needed to get out of there as soon as possible.

"You cannot stay here, Andy. We have to leave."

"But…Where?"

"To my house, of course. I cannot leave you here like this." Frank stood up and gave Andy a hand. "Let's get out of here!"

"Frank…" Andy got up slowly, groaning in pain. "What is going to happen to my mom? She can't survive without me."

Frank thought, *he is unbelievable…* He looked at Andy and said, "She survived two weeks without your help while you are locked up here, I think she can do another two weeks without you."

"How about Love?" Andy was limping as they walked to the door. He seemed more worried about his mom and Love than himself.

Frank sighed. "Love can't come, remember. She doesn't exist on my side."

"But Frank…"

"I don't want to hear any other excuses Andy. We are leaving. Let's discuss this in Aurora Shell, OK?" Frank was impatient to leave this terrible house.

They started walking down the gloomy hall, their eyes set on the mom's bedroom. Love lead the way, as if she was making sure that they would get to the room OK. Andy was so weak that

Frank had to help him walk. When they got to Andy's room, Frank pulled some books from Andy's shelf and piled them up in front of the poster, so that Andy could easily climb up. Andy climbed up crying in pain.

"Come on Frank," he said.

"Wait a minute, I'm putting your books back," Frank replied.

"Who the hell are you?" a scratchy woman voice said.

Andy's mom was at the door. Her fake blonde hair was so messy that looked like the end of a broom. Her white nightgown was stained and definitely needed a good wash. Her face looked much older than her age. Her brown eyes were almost lifeless but still somehow cruel. She was holding a cigarette in her hand.

Frank was frozen. He didn't know what to do or what to say.

Andy's mom raised her voice, "How did you get out of that room! I had locked you in there! You little…." Suddenly, Love jumped on her face, and she yelled in pain. "Zazingo cat!"

"Frank, hurry!" Andy begged.

Frank ran across the room and climbed up into the wormhole. He pulled the Big Bang poster firmly down behind him, hoping that the flimsy paper would at least buy them a few extra seconds if Andy's mom tried to follow them. As he hurried through the tunnel after his friend, he could still hear her yelling. "Come back here, Andy! Where the hell you think you are going?! I'm not done with you!"

When they arrived at last in Aurora Shell, they were terrified with the idea that she could come through the wormhole and punish them. They stuck down the Big Bang poster tightly and stared at it for a horrifying couple of minutes, but nothing happened.

"I guess the time stopped there because we are both here?" Frank said.

"Well…that works for me," Andy said.

"Are you hungry? You must be starving," Frank asked.

"I thought you'd never ask," Andy smiled.

Frank was happy to see his friend smiling again. He went downstairs and made two peanut butter and jelly sandwiches for his friend. He poured some chocolate milk also. After Andy finished his food, Frank gave him clean pajamas. They were a little short for him, but for now, they would work. He prepared a very nice bed in Aurora Shell for Andy. He especially puffed the cushions for him. He gave him his favorite *Star Wars* blanket and some Band-Aids for his wounds.

"Do you need anything else, friend?" Frank asked.

Andy shook his head. "No, thanks." Then he pulled his blanket over himself. "Frank?"

"Yes?"

"What am I going to do now?" his voice was shaky.

"Now you will sleep, and tomorrow we will make a plan. Don't worry. I'm here."

"I'm so lucky to have you, my friend. You saved my life."

"Well, you saved my life many times during our adventure, remember?"

Andy smiled. "I guess so. I did, didn't I?"

"Have a good night Andy. Sleep well. Tomorrow is a new day…Kokoronko!"

"Hahaha!" He felt some pain in his chest while laughing. "Ouch…Kokoronko to you too!"

Frank spent all night coming up with a perfect plan. He would try to make his dream come true. Early in the morning – so early that his parents were still asleep- he went to Aurora Shell and woke Andy up to tell him about the plan.

Joy filled Andy's eyes at first, but then it turned to sadness very quickly. "That's crazy!" Andy said, "They would never accept me. Why would they?"

"You don't know them. They are really nice." Frank smiled with hope. "And besides, I'm sure they'll like you right away, you are funny."

"Yeah, well. I don't know about that. It didn't work on my own mother."

"Come on, get up. We need to go downstairs and make breakfast."

"Together?" Andy was in shock.

"Together," Frank smiled. "Like two brothers!"

"But Frank, how are you going to explain where I came from?"

"I told you my plan. Just stick to it. You won't have to say a word, I will do everything."

"How about the wormhole? What if my mother finds a way to get in there?" Andy asked in fear.

"I've also found a solution for it. But I'll tell you later. Now, get up!"

"Oh, I have a very bad feeling about this, Frank."

"You always do, no worries. Come on, get up!"

They both went downstairs. Frank realized Andy's limp was even worse today. He pulled the chair out for him at the table. Andy slowly sat down, getting help from the table. After he sat down, he held his elbow.

"What's wrong with your arm?"

"I don't know. I guess it happened when mom first pushed me in the room. I fell on it."

"You need to see a doctor, Andy." Frank took some eggs and butter out of the fridge. "I'm sure my parents can take you to my doctor! Dr. Harrison is awesome! He fixes everything, and he gives me a medical journal every time I go there." Now Frank grabbed the frying pan from the lower cupboard under the sink. "But the journals are usually pretty hard to understand. Even for me. So, I usually just look at the photos and the image captions."

"Hey what is that?" Andy was pointing at the pancake mix on the counter.

"Oh, did you want pancakes instead?"

"What is a pancake?"

"Dude! You don't know what pancake is?!" Frank grabbed his face with both hands and murmured, "I can't believe this... You are missing out on so much in that universe!"

Andy laughed.

"What are you laughing at?"

"I was just kidding, of course we have pancakes. It was on the diner menu, too. Don't you remember?"

"Not funny."

"Frank? Who are you talking to?" Francine called from upstairs.

Andy looked at Frank with his eyes wide open. Frank moved his lips saying, "It's OK."

They could see her coming downstairs. She was wearing her light purple PJs and her bunny slippers. Frank and Joe had bought those for her last birthday. She was yawning when she saw Andy at the table. She stopped in the middle of the stairs and looked right at Frank with surprise.

"Mom, meet my friend, Andy."

"Oh..." Francine couldn't hide her amazement. "Nice to meet you Andy. What a nice surprise."

When Andy turned his back to look at Francine, she saw his face. It made her gasp. "Oh, my goodness! What happened to you?" She ran to Andy and sat in the chair next to him. "Let me look at you, it won't hurt, OK. sweetie?"

Andy nodded.

"Frank, do you know where the first aid kit is in the bathroom?"

"Umm…No?"

"OK. It is in the cupboard where we keep clean towels. Can you bring it to me?"

"Sure!" Frank ran upstairs.

"You don't have to run, honey!" Francine yelled from downstairs.

Frank found the kit in cupboard and ran back downstairs.

"Here," he said, leaving the kit on the table.

"OK. Let's see…" Francine open the kit; she was looking for something. "So, tell me what happened, Andy. Did you get in a fight at the school?"

"No ma'am," Andy replied. Andy was looking at Frank, as if asking for help.

Francine found what she had been looking for, a small tube of some kind of ointment. She opened it and started applying the cream to Andy's wounds carefully. "It's OK, you can tell me the truth. And you can call me Francine or Ms. Middleton." She looked at him and smiled.

"His mother did this," Frank said. "She is a mean person. She locked him in a room for two weeks!"

Francine immediately turned her head and looked at Frank as if she wanted to see if he was joking. But when she realized it wasn't a joke, her eyes were filled with an instant sadness and her mouth opened with awe, not knowing what to say. She turned back to Andy and looked at him with worried eyes. She gently stroked his hair. "Is this true, Andy?"

Andy nodded and looked down. Tears welled up in his eyes. Single teardrop streamed down his face, stopped at his chin for a second, and then fell on the kitchen floor. Everyone was so quiet that they all heard the teardrop splashing on the ground.

"Oh, honey. I'm so sorry!" Francine hugged Andy firmly. "How could a mother ever do that to her child?" She got up quickly and asked what any mother would ask, "OK. Now, did you already eat something?" Francine put the ointment back into the First Aid kit and locked it.

"I was making eggs and bacon," said Frank proudly.

"I can take over that. You guys just sit here," Francine took the frying pan and noticed the box of mix on the counter. "Anyone want pancakes?"

Both Andy and Frank raised their hands and smiled. Francine smiled back and walked to the fridge to get some more butter.

Just like in my dream! We are like a family, Frank thought. He didn't remember being this happy in a long time, he had a silly smile on his face the whole time. The pancakes, bacon and eggs were done twenty minutes later, and Frank, his mom, and Andy ate and talked together. Frank's dad joined them later. He looked as confused and worried as Francine. They whispered to each other at the table from time to time.

"I thought it was rude to whisper at the table when there are other people present," Frank said.

Joe cleared his throat. "Ahem…That is true, Frank. We apologize." He wiped his mouth with a napkin. "Andy, what time did you come here? I didn't hear the doorbell."

Andy looked at Frank. Frank jumped into the conversation. "It was very early. He knocked on the door. He said he was running away from his mom who was really mean to him."

"I see," Joe said, "I think you need a ride to school too, huh, champ?"

Andy looked at Frank again. Then he looked at Joe. "Thank you, Mr. Middleton!" Andy looked at Frank and then looked at Joe again. "But I don't really feel well. I would like to stay here if that's OK."

"I want to stay here too!" Frank said.

Joe crossed his eyebrows and took a sip of his coffee. "Hmm. I don't see a problem with you staying here, Andy. But your family must be really worried. We should let them know."

"No! Please no! She would hurt me again!" Andy got up from his chair so quickly that he almost lost his balance and fell. He groaned in pain while cradling his elbow.

Joe looked at Francine. She shrugged. "OK. Frank take Andy and go to your bedroom. Your father and I need to talk."

Frank and Andy went upstairs. Frank closed his bedroom door.

Andy was freaking out. "What are we going to do Frank? I don't even have an address or school here." Andy sat on Frank's bed. "Maybe I should have never left home. Maybe I should go back."

"Don't even think about it!" said Frank, "I saw what she did to you, Andy. You can't go back there."

"But what if your parents send me somewhere even worse?"

Frank was pacing up and down in the room, trying to guess what his parents were talking about downstairs. Something didn't seem right. They were definitely not giving the reaction he'd hoped for. He'd been sure that his parents would take one look at a kid who needed their help and offer to adopt him, too – and Frank would have a brother at last, and they would all be so happy.

A couple of times he opened his door and tried to listen but they weren't talking very loudly. *I wish I could hear what they are saying for once!* Frank thought.

Little while later, Francine came upstairs, knocked on Frank's door. When Frank answered her knock, Francine came in and said, "Get your backpack Frank, we are taking you to the school."

"What about Andy?" said Frank with worry. He glanced over at Andy, who was looking at his mom with huge, frightened eyes.

"Your father and I will take Andy somewhere we can get help."

"But…" Andy couldn't finish his sentence.

"Don't you worry, we are not taking you home, OK.?"

Frank couldn't keep it inside anymore. "Can't you just adopt him? You always tell me that you wanted to give me a brother or sister. I want him to be my brother. He needs a family. You love me, you care about me, you always want the best for me. Andy deserves that, too. Please, please, please, can he please stay with us?"

Francine had clearly not expected to hear any of this. She was speechless for a few seconds, thinking how to react. She obviously didn't want to hurt Frank's feelings. "Sweetie, I understand you, I really do. But things are complicated in adults' lives. It is not that easy."

"Why not?" Now Frank was raising his voice. "He needs a home, and I need a brother!"

"Frank Middleton, watch your tone. We're doing our best to help, and I don't like the way you're speaking to me." Francine was trying to keep everything under control.

"What is happening here?" Joe came into the room. "I have been waiting for you downstairs. We will be late."

Frank was really upset. In his mind, everything had such simple solutions. Why did adults have to make everything so complicated?

Andy, on the other hand, was just watching this heated conversation between a mother and her son, standing in the middle of the room not being able to look either of them in the eye. His palms were sweating, which didn't stop him from biting his nails. Thoughts of losing his home and his cat rushed in and made him really uncomfortable. He rocked his body unintentionally to calm himself down. Frank knew his friend well. *He must feel guilty about leaving his mom behind and he must be so scared*, he thought. But as he always did, Andy focused on the positive and said, "This was the best breakfast I had in my life Mrs. Middleton, thank you," and he gave Francine a big, though shaky, smile.

Francine responded with a gentle smile of her own. "You are welcome Andy." She didn't know what to think or what else to say. "Let's go kids, we have things to do."

They all got ready to leave the house. Frank lent some of his clothes to Andy, in which he looked absolutely hilarious. They all got into Joe's pickup.

"Buckle up, boys!" Joe yelled from the front seat.

Frank was so upset that he didn't even say a word in the car. Andy put his hand on Frank's shoulder and whispered, "It's all going to be OK. Frank. Don't worry!" He said. "Your parents are nice people."

Frank refused to talk during the ride and kept watching outside. When they dropped him off, he muttered a weak "Bye," to his parents and told Andy, "Well, I hope I will see you soon." The last thing he saw was Andy waving at him from the rear window, as their pickup left the parking lot.

11

ANDY'S DESTINY

Francine, Joe and Andy were alone in the car. There was an awkward silence that Andy didn't know how to break. He was usually good with these kinds of situations but was afraid to say something about his universe or his family and ruin everything. He felt like this would be a terrible time to make such a mistake.

"So, Andy," Joe said, "what is your favorite subject at school? Do you like science, like Frank?"

"I like science but not as much as Frank does, for sure."

Both Joe and Francine laughed.

Andy continued, "I like the practical skills class. They teach you everything from cooking to fixing chairs and cleaning the fire place."

"Oh, wow!" Francine was surprised, "I didn't know Frank's school offered classes like that. It sounds wonderful! Who is the teacher?"

There it was. He had already made a mistake. What was he going to say now?

"Mr. Tucker."

"Mr. Tucker? Hmm I don't think I remember him from the meetings," Francine said.

"Yeah, it's a pretty big school." Andy smiled nervously. "May I ask where we are going?"

Joe and Francine looked at each other.

"Sorry, Andy. We never told you what we are doing," Joe said. "We were just so taken by surprise with your story that we forgot to tell you. We are taking you to the Social Services Office. We have decided that this is the best thing to do."

Andy's smile was gone. His mouth was dry, blood was pounding in his ears. He was so scared that he was having a hard time hiding his fear. "I see. I could go myself though, you…You really don't have to drive me there."

"You are just eleven, Andy. We can't do that. Also, clearly Frank really likes you. We really want to help you," said Joe.

"Thanks," Andy said, still nervous. He thought to himself, *I'm in such trouble, oh God!*

Andy could imagine the chaos: They were going to take him to the Social Services Office, and when they couldn't find his records it would become obvious that he was lying! He thought about running away once they stopped the car. He could open the door and just run. But then, where would he go? Maybe somehow, he could sneak in Frank's house and go back to his universe through the wormhole. Maybe he could stay at his friend's house. Lamonte, the kid in his soccer team was his close friend. He would let him stay with him. But then his mother would tell Andy's mother where he was. Then for sure this time Andy's mother would kill him.

"I can see you are scared, Andy." Joe said. His and Andy's eyes met in the rearview mirror.

"I...I am a little worried." Andy had a hard time keeping his eye contact. "My family are not nice people."

Joe and Francine looked at each other again.

"What did they do to you, darling?" Francine asked very kindly.

Andy really wanted to say the things he went through. But he didn't know how to say it. It was painful to even think about them. "Mom drinks a lot; most of the time she is not sober. She rarely remembers to cook or clean. I do most of the cooking and cleaning in the house. I cook for her also. I'm worried about her. She is so skinny."

Both Joe and Francine were so sad about what they have just heard.

"Did really your mom do this to you? I mean, your face and the wounds on your arms?" Francine touched his hand gently.

Andy nodded.

"Oh, boy!" Joe said in an upset tone of voice. "I still can't believe this. How can you do this to a child?"

Andy somehow felt the courage to continue. "Two weeks ago, or so, I made her really mad, and she locked me in this room for more than ten days with my cat. She gave me food once a day, and she didn't even let me go to bathroom much."

Upon hearing this, Joe immediately pulled the car over onto the shoulder of the highway, too upset to drive. Cars sped past them where they sat. He looked at Francine. "I can't believe this. This is a crime! We need to report these people. They shouldn't get away with this."

"I know, honey," Francine replied, "And we will. This is why we are going to social services. Let's get there, first. Then we can make our formal complaints." She turned to Andy who was sitting in the back seat and said gently, "Andy, sweetheart, I'm so sorry that these horrible things happened to you. You are a great kid, and any family would feel lucky to have you as their child."

Andy thought to himself, *but you didn't...* He felt heartbroken. Frank had gotten Andy's hopes up. Andy had started to feel like finally he could have a loving family who cared for him. But the only thing Joe and Francine were doing was to take him to social services. He felt a little frustrated towards Frank. Because his plan clearly did not work. They should have worked together on a better plan, or a plan B. But it was too late now.

Joe started the car. "We definitely will figure this out Andy, nobody will hurt you again, we'll make sure of that."

Andy now could see what Frank liked about his father. He was definitely very protective and very strong. Andy had never known his own father, but he felt like he would be so proud if he had a father like Joe.

Eventually, they pulled back onto the highway and continued to drive in silence. They reached their exit and drove for a while on city streets before Joe pulled up next to a small and boring-looking government building. *Looks like a post office,* Andy thought, *except the fact that post offices always have long lines in front of the door. This place looks quiet.*

"Come on," said Joe, "You can come in with us."

Andy closed the pickup door. Francine took one of his hands and Joe took the other. They walked together towards the boring building.

They won't want to hold my hands once they figure out that I have no records here, Andy thought, *this was a mistake, I should have never left home.*

Once they entered the building, they found a large waiting area. The carpet had an old checkered pattern. With its pale brown and beige squares, it was so sad looking. Andy thought if carpets could speak this one would say, "I want to retire!" The blue plastic chairs had probably been there for decades. To their surprise, the place was completely empty.

"Hon, could you sit here with Andy? I will go check in at the front desk," Joe said.

Francine and Andy sat in the chairs by the big windows. She wrapped her left arm around him and gave him a kiss on the forehead. "Everything is going to be fine, don't be afraid, Andy." She stroked his hair with affection.

It was easier said than done, Andy thought. Andy was getting more and more uneasy about what was going to happen once they couldn't find his name in the database. For the first time in his life, he had no plan B.

Joe came back holding a paper. "Hey kiddo, do you have your ID with you by chance, or any kind of documentation?"

"Umm…No, unfortunately not," Andy shook his head.

"Can you tell me your home address?"

Yeah, same as yours, he thought to himself. "I don't remember the address, I'm sorry," he said, "We just had moved." He lied and he hated doing so.

"Oh, OK." Joe sounded frustrated. "What is your last name, Andy?"

And there it was again. After he said his last name, everything was going to be over. He thought about lying, but he had already told enough lies and it wouldn't make a difference anyways. "Carter," he said, "My name is Andrew Hayden Carter."

Joe wrote the name down on a piece of paper he was holding. "OK. Great. Francine, would you like to come with me? I feel like you might want to hear what they say, as well."

Francine nodded and turned to Andy. "Andy, honey, can you wait here until we come back?"

"Yeah, no problem."

"Are you sure? Would you like me to get you some water?"

"No, I'm good Mrs. Middleton, thank you."

"Aww…" Francine looked at Andy. "You are such a nice boy." She grabbed her coat and purse. "We will be right back."

Andy watched them leaving in slow motion. What was he going to do? Should he leave now? If he wanted to run, this was the perfect time for it. But then…What was he going to do after that? He wished Frank was with him. He would know what to do. Andy needed him so much.

Joe and Francine were welcomed by a big bald officer at the door. Andy was expecting him to have a uniform, but he wore black pants and a white button up shirt. His sleeves were folded and pulled up. He was wearing a striped red tie, but it looked like it was tied quickly and carelessly.

The officer closed the door and gently pulled out their chairs for them and then sat behind his desk. He clasped his hands in front of him and said, "Hello, my name is James Fischer. I'm an adoption social worker here. So, what brings you here today?"

"Mr. Fischer, we are here because we are worried about one of our son's friends."

"He said that he ran away from home because he was not treated well by his family. The stories that he's told us are horrifying," Francine said.

"Oh, I see," Mr. Fischer took a sip from his coffee, as if he needed the time to think what to say. "A lot of kids get angry at their parents every day for reasonable things like…Like taking away TV privileges, making them do chores, and most of the time they either overreact or try to get revenge on the parents somehow by making things up."

"Of course, but from what he has been telling us, there is definitely a bad treatment towards this child from his mother," Joe replied.

Mr. Fischer cleared his throat. "Ahem…I understand. But you also need to consider that children have great powers of imagination and…"

"Wait, are you implying that he might be lying?" Joe was upset. "The kid had a black eye and all sorts of bruises all over his body. I don't think he could have made all that up!"

Francine put her hand on Joe's knee, as a nice way of asking him to calm down. She continued for him in a much kinder way.

"We were just wondering if you could do something. We don't know if he is with a foster family or his own mother did this to him. Either way, we wanted to let you know about his situation," Francine said.

"Well…I can look him up in the system, but I'm afraid I cannot give you much information, since it is confidential."

"We understand that and we really appreciate your help." Francine smiled, holding Joe's hand tightly.

Mr. Fischer turned to his left with a deep sigh and started typing on his computer. He clicked on something, then he clicked again. Then he typed some more. "OK. What is the child's name?"

"Andrew Hayden Carter," said Joe, reading from the paper in his hand. Then he slipped it towards Mr. Fischer.

Andy was outside, nervously waiting to see what was going to happen. He decided not to leave but also not to talk once they come and ask him about the real story. What else could he do? Tell them about parallel universes, two Suns and the wormhole? How about disappearing cats? They would put him in a psych ward right away. He started biting his nails and walking up and down in the empty waiting area. Why was this taking so long?

"OK. I've found him," Mr. Fischer said, "I will print his record. Give me one second." He left the room, grabbed the print outs from the next room and came back. Joe and Francine were patiently waiting to hear Andy's story. Mr. Fischer was quietly skimming the papers and one could easily see that he wasn't happy about what he was reading.

"And?" Joe asked impatiently.

"So, Andrew Hayden Carter was brought to us about eleven years ago. They found him crying and hungry in front of the Central Hospital entrance. After they examined and gave the initial care, they sent him here. At the age of three, a foster family took him. At the age of six, he ran away and came back to us. Severe injuries around his neck were reported. Ahem…The next day, his foster family came and claimed that their biological child was jealous of him and they were having serious fights when they were not present in the room with them. Andrew did not say anything to defend himself so we sent him back home with them, thinking that this was only two brothers fighting each other." He turned the page. "Six months later there was a 911 call from the foster home that the father was beating the wife and children. As soon as we learned about this, we took Andrew out of that home. He spent two years in our institution without a family. Then, we finally found him another home. Two years after adoption, during our unannounced family visit, we found out that Andrew was essentially a prisoner in this family's home. He was cleaning, cooking for them. Also, he was forced to sleep on the couch and was not allowed to go to school…" Mr. Fischer sighed. It was easy to tell that he was getting more and more frustrated as he was reading Andy's file.

"Please go on," Joe said.

Francine's eyes were not able to hold the tears anymore. She was covering his mouth with her hand to hide her dismay.

"I...I had no idea..." Mr. Fischer looked at them in shock. He took a deep breath before he continued reading. "After that incident, a psychiatrist was assigned to Andrew and they met daily. The psychiatrist reported high level of intelligence and coping mechanism in Andrew. He was able to find something positive in everything negative. His final foster family took him two years ago and this family was actually a family that we had worked with before. So, we were sure that this time it was going to work." Mr. Fischer looked at the horrified couple. "But now, you are saying that he is not happy there, either."

"Absolutely not," Joe said, "He can't go back to that place. I want to believe that you are not going to let that happen."

Francine had not seen Joe this upset in a long time. She knew her husband. He was not going to leave that room without finding a solution.

"I want to assure you both that our institution always tries to do its best for these children–"

"So, what is going to happen next?" Francine interrupted. She was barely holding back her tears.

"Until we find an appropriate family for him, he will be staying with us. Once a family is available, and of course we do necessary background checks, then he will be staying with them."

"How about his school? This kid needs to go to school," said Joe firmly.

"We provide homeschooling here in our institution. It is for mixed age groups, but it is still better than no education."

A heavy stillness fell over them.

Andy was in the bathroom, washing his face when he heard his name being yelled "Andy!" He ran outside and saw Joe and Francine looking for him. Joe was smiling at him but Francine was in tears and a big bald guy was trying to say something behind them.

"We are leaving kiddo, let's go," Joe grabbed Andy's hand gently.

"What happened?" Andy was so confused. He thought, *they must have figured out that I'm lying. Is that why Mrs. Middleton crying? But this doesn't make sense.*

They got in the car and left the place in silence. Nobody talked during the ride, either. Andy thought, *they must be so angry that they don't know what to say.*

"Are you hungry?" Francine smiled at Andy.

"A little," Andy said, still bewildered.

"How about some chicken fingers and fries?"

Andy's eyes were wide open and his mouth was watering. "Yes, please!"

They stopped at one of these fast food restaurants that Andy had never seen before in his life. Inside, it smelled so good that he wanted to eat everything on the menu. After they got their food, they sat at a corner table. Everyone was so quiet. *This can't be good,* Andy thought. He took a big bite of his delicious fried chicken and asked, "So…What did they say?"

"We heard about your story Andy. I'm so sorry that you had to go through all those horrible experiences." Francine's eyes were tearful again.

Andy was confused. So, his name actually 'was' in the database? *Wow!* he thought, *what are the chances?! That means I was actually an orphan…*

"It is OK," said Andy and smiled. "Really. I'm happy now as we are together and that's what matters."

"This kid is special," Joe told Francine. "Are you always this positive?" he asked to Andy.

Andy shrugged. "Frank loves this side of me, too. Honestly, being negative never helped. But when I look at things positively, most of the time I feel better and things end up working out."

"He speaks like an adult," Francine told Joe, smiling.

"Seriously!" Joe said and got a big bite from his burger. "Come on now, eat your food, kiddo. Today Francine and I are not going to work. We are going to take you to the hospital first, get you checked up. Then, we will do some grocery shopping and head back home afterwards to cook dinner together. Would that sound good to you?"

Andy had the biggest smile on his face, so that his cheeks were hurting. Although he was still confused about what was going on and why he was still with them, he cared more about being in the moment. After a very long time, he felt loved and cared for. Actually, thinking about it, he had never felt this happy in his life before. Not even when his favorite soccer team had won the world championship. *So, this is what it feels like to have a real family!* he thought, *this is so wonderful!*

"Yeah, sure I would love to!" Andy replied, "Could we make some space cookies for Frank?"

"Space cookies?" Francine asked.

"Yeah! He always talks about how before Christmas you guys make solar system cookies together and he loves that."

Joe was amazed. "He told you that? I had no idea he loved them so much. Of course, we can definitely make some planet cookies, that's what we call them." He looked at his watch and said, "But now we need to get going because it is getting late. We have stuff to do."

After that small and boring Social Services building, the hospital looked huge and scary. It had two giant revolving doors through which either a doctor or patient was coming in and out every second. When they entered, the receptionist was just about to hang up the phone. She smiled at them and welcomed them warmly. She said the name of the hospital so fast that Andy couldn't catch it. Andy never liked hospitals. They always smelled too clean. A smell that reminds him bad memories. Once he had to call an ambulance when he found his mom not breathing on the kitchen floor. Another time she got pneumonia but couldn't leave the hospital for two weeks since she was a heavy smoker. Andy was the one who would bring her clean clothes and make sure she got what she needed on the expense of missing classes.

They took the elevator to the third floor. They were walking down in the hallway when an old man passing by waived at Andy from his wheelchair. Andy waived back at him with a smile. Joe opened the big glass door for Francine and Andy. He approached to the receptionist and talked to the gentleman at the desk. Andy heard him saying, "Doctor Lee will be with you shortly." They were sitting in the waiting area quietly when the doctor came with a toy space rocket in his hand. He couldn't pay attention to what the doctor said or asked for a while because his all focus was on that amazing toy.

When he sat on the exam chair, Dr. Lee gave the toy to Andy and smiled. "Hello, Andy. I'm Dr. Lee, very nice to meet you. Now, I will examine you, OK? If anything I do hurts or makes you uncomfortable, you'll immediately tell me, OK?"

Andy nodded.

While Dr. Lee was checking Andy's arms he asked, "Would you like to tell me what happened?"

Each time he remembered what happened to him, he wished he did not. To keep himself away from these negative feelings, he decided to treat his past like a bad reality TV show. The remote control was in his hands. So, whenever he felt upset, he could change the channel and tune in a happy moment like the ones with Frank.

"I could tell you that I fell of my bike, but I don't like lying," Andy said. "My mom punished me for something I did."

Dr. Lee didn't seem surprised and continued examining him.

"Is your mom the lady you came here with?"

"No. Mrs. Middleton is my best friend's mother. They took me to social services this morning."

"Ah, I see... That's very nice of them," said Dr. Lee.

After cleaning up his wounds, wrapping his elbow with an elastic bandage and writing a prescription, they sent Andy home. He had sprained his elbow and he just needed to be more careful about it from now on. On their way out, Andy heard Francine asking Joe, "Did you take care of it?" and Joe saying "Yeah, it's all good."

Once they got in the car, Andy understood what they were talking about. "Thank you, Mr. and Mrs. Middleton," he said, "I'm really grateful."

"No problem, kiddo. Are you buckled up?" asked Joe. Andy nodded. He remembered Frank talking about how his family was financially struggling. He really hoped that this hospital visit didn't caused so much trouble to Frank's family.

Next on the to do list was buying groceries. Andy had never thought that grocery shopping could be so much fun. Francine asked his opinion about brands and food options. Even though he had no idea most of the time, he felt like he was helping and his ideas were valued. He watched Joe sneaking some potato chips into the shopping cart. He whispered, "Don't tell Francine, she thinks I'm getting fat," making Andy giggle. They were in such a rush since they wanted to make sure the dinner was ready when Frank got home.

As soon as they arrived home, they went straight to kitchen. Francine was making an amazing mac and cheese casserole, meatloaf, and a very colorful looking salad. The casserole and meatloaf in the oven were making the kitchen smell like "home" for Andy. *This is how my grandparents' home used to smell during Christmas,* he remembered. Unfortunately, they lived very far away and his mom was no longer taking him there as they sold their car a few years back.

Baking was so much fun. Francine taught him some pointers. "You always need to preheat the oven before you bake anything." "Always beat the eggs before adding them to the dough." "Don't add icing if the cookies are still hot, let them cool a little bit first." "We need to spray some oil on the cookie sheet so that the cookies don't stick to the pan."

Andy almost wanted to take notes. He was afraid that he was going to forget everything. "How did you learn all this?"

"By trial and error, sometimes from recipe books. Sometimes just by experience," Francine smiled.

"I'm going to go pick up Frank," Joe said and gave Francine a kiss on the lips.

"Dinner should be ready by the time you guys get here. See you soon!" said Francine. She turned to Andy, "Do you want to see what is on TV until they get back?"

"Sure!" said Andy.

They started watching a show called *Jeopardy* on TV. Andy wasn't even paying attention to the questions. He was looking around, looking at Francine then looking at himself. He couldn't believe where he was, what he was doing and how happy he was. The only bad thing was that he missed his cat, Love. Then he felt so bad that he didn't miss his mom. He hoped that she was doing OK. He felt safer and happier here, with Francine, Joe and Frank. He was in a much better place.

12

FRANK'S DREAM

When Joe picked up Frank, he was still grumpy. He didn't say a word and Joe didn't say anything about the surprise at home. When they arrived home and got out of the car, finally Frank couldn't hold his tongue. "Did you send Andy back to his mother?"

"No. Don't worry Frank, nobody will hurt him again, we made sure of that." Joe smiled and opened the door with his keys.

"We are home!" said Joe.

When Frank entered the house and saw Andy sitting on the couch, he couldn't believe his eyes. "Andy?!" He ran to him without even taking off his shoes.

They hugged each other and laughed.

"Good to see you, friend," said Andy.

"Yes!" Frank said. He turned to his dad and said, "is he staying with us for dinner?"

Francine walked up right next to Joe and they held each other. Joe said, "Kids, we want to share something with you. But the food is ready and getting cold, let's talk about it while we are eating, okay?"

Andy started to feel the fear again, it was filling up his chest. Had they decided to give him to that bald guy? Had all that cooking and waiting for Frank to arrive been just to give him the bad news?

"Andy, are you coming?" asked Frank.

"Oh, sorry. Sure," Andy said. He sat right next to Frank at the table. Joe was sitting at the one end of the table and Francine was sitting at the other end.

"Give me your plate, hon," said Francine.

At that moment Joe's cell phone rang. "Excuse me," he said and left the table.

While Frank was passing his plate to his mother, Francine asked, "So, how was school?"

"Good, I guess…I got an A+ on my science paper today," Frank said.

"Oh baby, that's wonderful!" Francine said. "Congratulations!"

Andy gave a high five to Frank and patted him on the back.

"I'm glad you deserved those cookies then," Joe said, walking back into the kitchen, smiling. He put his cell phone back into his pocket.

"What cookies? You made cookies?" Frank's eyes opened wide.

"Not just cookies," Andy said while he was passing his plate to Francine. "They are planet cookies!"

"No way!" Frank jumped out of his chair and yelled, "Yessss!"

Now everyone had their delicious looking food in front of them. "Yay! Mac & cheese!" Frank was so excited and impatient about his dinner. *Just like in my dream*, Frank thought, *we are like a perfect family.*

While everyone else had dived into their food already, Joe hadn't touched his food yet as he was looking at Francine for a cue. After Francine gave the cue he was waiting for, he cleared his throat. "Ahem. Frank, as you know we took Andy somewhere today."

"Yeah. But I have no idea where!" Frank said and then ate a spoonful of mac and cheese. It was still so warm that almost burned his mouth.

"Well, we went to the Social Services Office to learn about Andy's story."

Frank dropped his spoon on his plate. "Social services? Isn't that the place that gives homeless children a place to stay?"

"Yes. Also, they arrange foster families, who want to give care to children."

He swallowed the mac and cheese in his mouth without even chewing. "OK." Frank looked at Andy, scared to hear what his father was about to say. And Andy was no different.

"I'm not going to explain in detail here what we talked about with Mr. Fischer." Joe took a sip of water. "He was the man in charge there. But…He proposed something and we accepted it." Joe put a forkful meat loaf and salad in his mouth upon finishing his sentence.

Everyone watched him as he chewed quietly. Frank couldn't wait anymore. "And?"

Joe cleaned his mouth with a napkin. "Ahem…So, he proposed that Andy could stay here with us, and we would be his foster parents. But we weren't sure until a few seconds ago if we could. They got our background check results, and they said that there is nothing that would prevent us from adopting you, Andy, as our son. They are getting the paperwork ready; we will go and sign them this week."

Frank and Andy looked at each other with so much excitement, the happiness was almost too much to bear. "Are you serious?" Frank asked his dad. If this was a joke, he didn't want to get frustrated.

"Hahaha we are telling the truth. We want to be Andy's family." Francine confirmed.

Andy started shaking and Frank couldn't sit still. He got off his chair and stared at his mom and dad as if he had just given him the biggest Christmas present ever. Andy and Frank turned and looked at each other with tears in their eyes. They hugged each other so firmly that Frank couldn't breathe for a second.

Then they both ran to Francine and hugged her first.

"Thank you, Mrs. Middleton!"

"Thank you, Mom, I love you!"

Then Joe joined them. It was a very long group hug with lots of kisses and hugs and tears.

"Ouch, Frank, my elbow!" Andy said in pain.

"Sorry!"

"We need to start eating, the food is getting cold," Francine said. She was still crying tears of joy.

Neither Andy nor Frank could believe what was happening at that moment. They were so happy that they thought they were in a dream or had somehow stumbled into a third universe or something. This was the best day ever for Frank. During dinner they laughed, talked and enjoyed the delicious food.

"Mom, Andy is stealing my dinner roll!" said Frank.

"Well, you guys are not losing anytime, are you? Already acting like brothers!" she smiled. "I have more dinner rolls in the oven, don't worry and just eat what you have in front of you."

From that moment on Andy and Frank were truly a family. They grew up together, went to school together and traveled together. But most importantly, they learned from each other a lot. Thanks to Andy, Frank became more sociable. He made many friends and had long lasting relationships. And thanks to

Frank, Andy learned how the power of knowledge makes some-one brave. Going to the museums, camps and field trips with Frank became the most enjoyable activity of Andy's.

They never told Joe and Francine anything about the wormhole or Andy being from another universe. Andy had his own room but he spent most of his time in Frank's room as an old habit. They were not hanging out in Aurora Shell anymore as they had found each other and they didn't feel the need to hide. Andy thought about his mother sometimes, worried about her. But he never had the courage to go back to checkup on her. He also wished he could have had Love with him but he knew it was impossible. He wished they were both in a better place now, just like he was.

Joe and Francine loved Andy as much as they loved Frank. Frank never told his parents that he knew he was adopted. But when he turned 18, Joe and Francine told him anyway. There were tears, and hugs. Frank acted like he was surprised and he thought he was pretty successful at it. Nevertheless, he appreci-ated the fact that they finally had told him.

Exploring this universe was difficult but fun for Andy. For example, people were overly excited about this game called baseball, for him it was super boring. He loved Thanksgiving, which he never had heard before. Andy's universe had something similar, but it was called "Family Day." Everyone would be off that day to be with their family and eat a big dinner.

Andy was amazed by dinosaurs. After he learned that they were extinct, he felt terrible and actually missed seeing Konggongs although he was still terrified of them. One thing very difficult for him in high school was having a date. It seemed so easy at first as he was a very friendly and sociable person. However, as the conversation moved along, he would realize he didn't know most of the things his date was referring to like TV shows, some old jokes, proverbs or historical things. They were difficult for him to know as he had been trying to catch up with this universe only for a few years. He always thought he looked illiterate or stupid. So, he worked hard to learn about history and the popular culture; not just to impress girls but also not to stand out in the crowd.

Andy didn't know but Frank was always watching his back just to make sure he was not putting himself in dangerous situations. Frank would teach him about their universe each time they went out to explore. Frank realized he learned better when he taught things. Once he taught Andy how to make a space rocket from Legos. That one was the best he ever did. In every museum, Frank told Andy about the story behind the exhibit: "This is an Egyptian mummy from 2400 BC. It looks like it was taken from the burial site of 5th Dynasty Egyptian Pharaoh Unis's son Unis-Ankh." "Oh, this fossil is called a Trilobite, which are one of the first animals in the fossil record to develop complex eyes; you can find millions of them in Utah." "There you go, this is a mineral called 'Pyrite.' It is also called 'fool's gold' because it looks a lot like gold. Do you see the cubical forms? Those are not man-made. Pyrites are found in cubic forms in nature. Amazing, huh?" Frank was Andy's tour guide, guardian angel and his hero at the same time with his bravery and wisdom.

Some days Andy thought about other Andy, who was an orphan. He wondered how he was doing, where he lived in this universe. He wished he could help. But Andy was afraid to make things complicated. So, he decided that the best thing to do was to bury the matter, forever.

Both Andy and Frank still talked about the wormhole and the magic of Big Bang posters sometimes. They wondered how the two same posters opened a wormhole between the two universes? Today, as a space engineer, even Frank hasn't figured it out yet.

And the wormhole…It has been sealed for good. When Frank and Andy turned 16, they realized that this wormhole could create a problem if their parents found out. So, during their three-day anniversary weekend while Francine and Joe were away, they filled it in with bricks from end to end. They filled up the empty spaces with concrete. As he was blocking the only way back to his old universe, Andy felt bittersweet. He said goodbye to his mom, Love, friends at school, and his grandparents. He tried to think a nice memory with each one of them as he laid bricks on top of each other. Once it was finished, they painted the wall in Aurora Shell. It was still recognizable, but it didn't look too obvious, either.

Before Frank moved to another city for college, he had cleaned his room and gave some stuff away, but he had kept the Big Bang poster. Then he learned a few years later that his mother had sold the poster to someone random during a garage sale. Since then, he has been wondering about the same thing: *How many lives has that poster must have changed so far? and how many will it continue to change? I hope everyone turns out to be as lucky as I am*, Frank thought.

Because, my dream of a perfect family has come true.

The End

Frank